"Your Son?" Mac Repeated.

Rachel hiked up her chin. "That's right," she told him. "*My* son."

Still reeling from the shock of discovering Rachel had a child, Mac looked from her to the dark-haired boy in her arms and back again. Rachel's son and his, Mac realized as he stared into eyes identical to his own.

He had a son. A son!

Suddenly shock gave way to temper as the reality of the situation hit him. He kept his eyes trained on Rachel's face. And even though he already suspected he knew the answer, he asked her anyway, "How old is he?"

"He's eighteen months."

Mac didn't have to be a math wizard to figure out that Rachel had been pregnant when he had left New Orleans. *Had she known then?* Doing his best to control the emotions slamming through him, Mac, said, "Which means that he's mine. I'm his father."

Dear Reader,

Ring in the New Year with the hottest new love stories from Silhouette Desire! *The Redemption of Jefferson Cade* by BJ James is our MAN OF THE MONTH. In this latest installment of MEN OF BELLE TERRE, the youngest Cade overcomes both external and internal obstacles to regain his lost love. And be sure to read the launch book in Desire's first yearlong continuity series, DYNASTIES: THE CONNELLYS. In *Tall, Dark & Royal*, bestselling author Leanne Banks introduces a prominent Chicago family linked to European royals.

Anne Marie Winston offers another winner with *Billionaire Bachelors: Ryan*, a BABY BANK story featuring twin babies. In *The Tycoon's Temptation* by Katherine Garbera, a jaded billionaire discovers the greater rewards of love, while Kristi Gold's *Dr. Dangerous* discovers he's addicted to a certain physical therapist's personal approach to healing in this launch book of Kristi's MARRYING AN M.D. miniseries. And Metsy Hingle bring us *Navy SEAL Dad*, a BACHELORS & BABIES story.

Start the year off right by savoring all six of these passionate, powerful and provocative romances from Silhouette Desire!

Enjoy!

Joan Marlow Golan

Joan Marlow Golan
Senior Editor, Silhouette Desire

Please address questions and book requests to:
Silhouette Reader Service
U.S.: 3010 Walden Ave., P.O. Box 1325, Buffalo, NY 14269
Canadian: P.O. Box 609, Fort Erie, Ont. L2A 5X3

Navy SEAL Dad

METSY HINGLE

Silhouette® Desire®

Published by Silhouette Books

America's Publisher of Contemporary Romance

 SILHOUETTE BOOKS

ISBN 0-373-76416-2

NAVY SEAL DAD

This edition published by arrangement with Harlequin Books S.A.

® and TM are trademarks of Harlequin Books S.A., used under license.
Trademarks indicated with ® are registered in the United States Patent
and Trademark Office, the Canadian Trade Marks Office and in other
countries.

Visit Silhouette at www.eHarlequin.com

Printed in U.S.A.

METSY HINGLE

celebrated her tenth book for Silhouette with the publication of *The Baby Bonus*. Metsy is an award-winning, bestselling author of romance who resides across the lake from her native New Orleans. Married for more than twenty years to her own hero, she is the busy mother of four children. She recently traded in her business suits and a fast-paced life in the hotel and public-relations arena to pursue writing full-time. Metsy has a strong belief in the power of love and romance. She also believes in happy endings, which she continues to demonstrate with each new story she writes. She loves hearing from readers. For a free doorknob hanger or bookmark, write to Metsy at P.O. Box 3224, Covington, LA 70433.

One

He was back!

Rachel Grant's heart slammed against her chest as she stared at the back of the tall, dark-haired man in Navy dress whites standing at the nurses' station. Barely able to breathe, she stood frozen outside of the hospital room she'd been about to enter. Lifting her gaze from the wide shoulders that spanned the military jacket, she noted the wave of jet black hair at his nape that defied the close-cropped style.

Sweet heavens, it *was* Mac!

But it couldn't be Mac, she reasoned as she tried to quell her racing pulse. The last she'd heard, Lieutenant Commander Pete "Mac" McKenna was a million miles away in one of those foreign countries with an unpronounceable name doing his macho Navy SEAL thing. Besides even if Mac were stateside again, he wouldn't return to New Orleans. Why should he? He'd made it

painfully clear two years ago that a long-term relationship
with her didn't fit in with his plans. A sharp pain sliced
through Rachel at the memory of what a fool she had
made of herself over Mac McKenna. Even after all this
time, her blindness where he had been concerned still
smarted. Thank heavens for pride, she thought. It was all
that had saved her from making an even bigger fool of
herself and pleading with him not to shut her out of his
life.

At the ding of the elevator Rachel gave her head a
shake and dragged her thoughts away from the past. Dismissing the notion that the man was Mac, she chided
herself silently for the foolish lapse. Of course the man
wasn't Mac. It had been the uniform and dark hair that
had thrown her off. That and the bout of nerves she'd
been battling since Alex had begun dropping hints about
marriage. It was only natural that thoughts of marriage
would cause her to think of Mac. After all, there had been
a time not very long ago when she had hoped that he
would be asking her to marry him.

She pressed a fist to her breast, hating the fact that
even after more than two years, Mac's not wanting her
could still cause her pain. Irritated with herself, Rachel
scowled. She had more important things to do than mull
over her failed relationship with Mac McKenna, she reminded herself. Important things like her job—which in-
cluded reassuring Mr. Goldblum about his gall bladder
surgery in the morning. Snatching the patient chart and
clipboard from the door, Rachel scanned the doctor's
notes.

"I'm looking for one of your nurses—Rachel Grant. I
was told I could find her up here."

The air backed up in Rachel's lungs at the sound of
that deep, rumbling voice. And for the space of a heart-

beat she couldn't breathe. Her heart racing, she swung her gaze back to the Navy officer. No! It couldn't be Mac. Not now. Not after all this time.

"She's probably in with a patient at the moment. Is there something I can help you with?"

"Then she does still work here?"

Dear God, it *was* Mac!

In her distress she must have made some sound, Rachel realized. Or maybe Mac simply had sensed her presence as he'd always had such an uncanny knack for doing in the past. Whatever the reason, Rachel stood frozen as he whirled around and looked in her direction.

"Rachel!"

She could feel the blood drain from her cheeks as she saw his face—the face that had haunted her for all those months after he'd gone. Too stunned to move, she simply stood there and stared at him. He hasn't changed. The ridiculous thought flitted through her brain as he started toward her. Same stubborn jaw. Same sharp cheekbones. Same sexy mouth that had been able to make her toes curl when he smiled at her. The way he was smiling at her now.

"Rach, I can't believe I actually found you," he said, skimming his gaze over her like a jungle cat who was sizing up his next meal. Trapped in the intensity of his blue eyes, Rachel didn't even realize Mac had reached for her until she found herself wrapped in his arms. "God...it's so good to see you again. And you look...you look wonderful."

"I...so do you," she replied, too shaken to even realize how lame the words sounded. And before she could register his intent, Mac's lips were on hers. Warm. Gentle. Hungry. Familiar.

The taste and scent of him, the feel of his body pressed

against hers after so long, struck some cold, empty place deep inside Rachel, a part of her that she had buried beneath an ocean of tears and heartache. The sound of the clipboard striking the tile floor echoed like thunder in Rachel's ears. She jerked her mouth free.

She took one shaky step back. And then another. "The chart," she murmured inanely. Feeling dazed, she stooped down to retrieve the patient chart and folder with less than steady fingers. As she did so, she attempted to marshal the emotions ricocheting through her.

"Here, let me get that for you," Mac offered, flashing her one of those grins that did nothing to help her equilibrium.

When he knelt down beside her and began scooping up the papers that had fallen from her folder, Rachel stood. Finally the noises of the hospital managed to penetrate her senses. She glanced toward the nurses' station and nearly groaned at the speculative looks being cast in her direction.

"Here you go," Mac said, handing her the papers.

Taking the papers from him, she quickly shoved everything into the folder and hugged it and the chart to her. "Thanks," she said, and nearly winced at how stiff and formal she sounded—particularly when the man had just kissed her.

"No problem," Mac told her, and as though sensing her uneasiness, the grin tugging at his mouth faded. "I meant what I said, Rach. You have no idea how glad I am to see you. And you really do look good. Better than good, you're even more beautiful than I remembered."

"I see you found Ms. Grant," the young nursing assistant who'd been manning the station desk addressed Mac.

He flashed the younger woman one of his megawatt smiles. "Yes, ma'am. I sure did. Thanks for your help."

The other woman beamed. "Anytime."

Noting the dreamy look on the younger woman's face, Rachel beat back an unexpected stab of jealousy. She had no right to be jealous, Rachel reminded herself. She had no claim on Mac. She never had. Even when they'd been together, he'd never really been hers. The fact that she'd made the mistake of falling in love with him hadn't been Mac's problem. It had been hers and hers alone. Just as the unexpected dividend of their short-term affair had been hers alone. Her heart swelled as she thought of little P.J. and how much he had changed her life.

P.J.!

Panic shot through Rachel like a bullet as she stared at Mac, worried over the impact his appearance might cause on their lives.

"I'll remember that, Kimberly," Mac said, reading the woman's name tag. "And thanks again."

"Like I said, anytime, Commander," she replied, and after a brief nod to Rachel, she hurried over to the nurses' station where a phone line was ringing.

Commander? Rachel yanked her attention to the gold bars on Mac's uniform. "I didn't realize you'd been promoted."

He shrugged. "A couple of months ago."

"Congratulations, Mac."

"Thanks."

"I'm happy for you." And she was, Rachel realized. She knew how much Mac's career meant to him. She'd discovered just how important it was when he'd informed her that he was leaving and didn't know when or if he'd be back. While he'd revealed little to her about what his activities as a SEAL entailed, she had learned enough about the elite military unit to know that the missions Mac and his team undertook weren't without danger or risk. Besides, Mac had been honest with her—brutally so the last time she'd seen him. He'd told her not to wait for him, because he could never offer her what she deserved—a commitment, a family, a future. But the bottom line was that Mac hadn't wanted those things with her. Or at least not enough to try. For him, it came down to a choice—the SEALs or her. And he'd chosen the SEALs.

"I've missed you, Rach," he said, his eyes darkening. It reminded her of the way Mac had looked at her the first time they'd made love…as though she was the only thing in the world that mattered to him. He lifted his hand, stroked his knuckles along her cheek the way he had countless times when they'd been together.

His touch, his smell, the look in his eyes brought everything back to Rachel in a rush. And it seemed like only yesterday that she had lain naked in his arms, her heart filled with love and dreams. But Mac hadn't wanted her love. Her dreams hadn't been his, she reminded herself. Resenting the fact that just the memory still had the power to make her heart ache this way, Rachel took a step back.

"I'm sorry," he said, his hand falling to his side. "I guess I shouldn't have just shown up here like this without any warning. But I wasn't even sure if I was going to make the trip to New Orleans until I was practically on the plane. Then once I got here, all I could think of was that I had to see you, find out how you were doing."

Of course, he'd wanted to see her again. Why wouldn't he? She'd been quite an accommodating playmate for him the last time he'd been in town, hadn't she? Pain and bitterness rose like bile in her throat. "As you can see, I'm doing just fine," she told him.

"I can see that," he said, his eyes sparkling with appreciation. "I tried to reach you when I got in yesterday evening, but your old phone number had been disconnected. I went by your apartment, but I was told you'd moved. That's when I decided to come by the hospital and see if you still worked here." He gave her that lopsided grin. "Lucky for me you didn't change jobs, too."

"You know me, Mac. Predictable as always. I'll probably still be here twenty years from now and the next time you're passing through," she said, unable to keep the sharpness out of her tone.

Mac narrowed his eyes. "It wasn't a put-down. I've always admired your dedication to your job. It was one of the things that attracted me to you—the fact that you always knew you wanted to be a nurse just like I knew I wanted to be a SEAL. It's one of the things we have in common."

She couldn't help but feel a slash of pain as she thought about how much more they had in common than he knew. Yet the idea of telling him about P.J. now, sent panic racing through her blood. "I... It was good to see you again, Mac. But I really need to get back to work." Ignoring the look of confusion that crossed his handsome face, she started past him.

"Hang on a second," he said, blocking her path.

"Mac, I told you, I have to get back to work."

"I know." He frowned, watched her out of eyes she was afraid would see too much. "Listen, I'm not sure what I said to upset you, but whatever it is, I do apologize."

"Fine. Now if you'll excuse me." She started past him a second time. Mac mirrored her actions and once again blocked her path. "I told you, I need to get back to work."

"Take a break."

"I don't want a break," she countered.

"Take one, anyway. I want to talk to you."

"Forgive me, but somehow I doubt talk is what you had in mind when you came here looking for me." And even as she said the words, Rachel knew she wasn't being fair. After all, why shouldn't he think she'd be ready to resume their affair, when she'd been so willing to take him to her bed the last time he'd been in town.

His blue eyes chilled, and there wasn't the hint of a smile in sight. "I have no problem doing this in front of an audience. We finish this conversation right here, right now, where everyone can hear us, or we can do it in private. It's your call, Rachel. What's it going to be?"

He meant it, Rachel realized, noting the stubborn set of his jaw. "I've only got a few minutes," she told him and led him to the staff lounge, which thankfully was empty. "All right, Mac," she said turning to face him. "We're alone now. So why don't you tell me why you're here."

He met her gaze, held it. "I'm here because I wanted…no, I needed to see you," he said with a grimness so at odds with the man she remembered.

During their four weeks together, Mac had laughed and loved with her with a boldness that stole her breath. He'd made her feel daring and exciting and sexy, nothing at all like dull-as-dishwater Rachel Grant the minister's daughter, who always followed the rules. She'd broken every rule she'd been taught and believed in about abstaining from premarital sex, about the need for love and commitment. And she'd broken them without regret, without shame. Until Mac had told her he was leaving, that there could be no future for them.

His expression softened. ''I meant what I said, Rach. I really have missed you.''

The words were like knives through her heart, resurrecting old feelings, old dreams, old hurts. ''What am I supposed to say to that, Mac?''

''I was hoping that maybe you missed me, too.''

Missing didn't come close to describing how she'd felt when he had left. She'd felt lost. Alone. Dead inside. Until she'd found out about P.J. Discovering she was pregnant with Mac's baby had been all that had kept her going those first few months. And now here Mac was again, back in New Orleans for a week or two, he'd said. So he'd decided to look her up.

''I guess I can't blame you for not believing me, but it's the truth. I never forgot you, Rachel.''

''Really? Is that why I haven't heard from you in over two years? No phone calls, no letters. Not even a postcard to say you were still alive.''

His mouth tightened. ''I never led you on, Rachel.''

''No, you didn't,'' she admitted, and the admission left her almost as raw now as it had two years ago. ''You made it clear when you left that it was over between us. I shouldn't have been surprised not to hear from you. But I was surprised.'' And hurt, she admitted silently.

''Rachel.'' He said her name softly, reached out to touch her face.

She turned away, not wanting him to see the pain in her eyes. Steeling herself against the feelings he stirred in her, she said, ''You'll have to forgive me, if I find your claim about missing me somewhat convenient.''

''Convenient?'' he repeated, genuine puzzlement in his voice. ''Just what is it you're accusing me of?''

Having regained some measure of control over her emotions, Rachel turned around to face him again. "I'm not accusing you of anything," she told him evenly. "I'm simply saying that after all this time without a word from you, you find yourself back in New Orleans and decide to look me up and tell me how much you've missed me."

"It's true."

"Is it? Or maybe you thought it was a good line and you'd use it to talk your way back into my bed. After all, I was pretty accommodating the last time you were in town," she said, unable to keep the bitterness from her voice. "So I guess I can understand why you might think I'd be interested in picking up things where we left off. And maybe I would be if—"

"Don't," he said the word softly, but there was no mistaking the steel behind the warning. She caught the icy glint of anger in those blue eyes. "I never used you, Rachel. Don't cheapen yourself or me by pretending that I did."

The truth of his statement shamed her. "You're right, of course. You never used me, Mac. You didn't have to. I allowed myself to be used."

"Rachel."

He reached for her, but Rachel stepped away. She turned her back to him, not wanting him to witness her shame. "You'll have to forgive me. Having your lover tell you to forget him…to go find yourself a nice guy with a safe, nine-to-five job to fall in love with has a way of making a woman feel particularly stupid." Hiking up her chin, she turned around to face him again. "But I'm a lot smarter than I used to be, Mac. Which brings us back to my question. Why are you here?"

"Because I didn't follow my own advice."

Rachel frowned. "What do you mean?"

He pinned her with hard blue eyes. "I mean I didn't forget *you*. I haven't been *able* to forget you—no matter how hard I've tried."

Rachel blinked, caught off guard as much by his reply as by the dark heat behind it. Emotions surged through her like a storm. Pleasure. Hope. Fear. But it was the fear and the memory of all those long and lonely months when she'd prayed for Mac to contact her, to tell her he wanted to give their love a chance that kept her anchored now. She was no longer a naive woman who could be easily swept off her feet by the handsome Navy SEAL. She was a single mother with responsibilities. And she couldn't afford to play emotional games with the likes of Mac McKenna.

"It's true. There hasn't been a single day in the past two years that I haven't thought about you."

Shaken, Rachel clutched the clipboard to her like a shield. "Why are you doing this?" she demanded, wanting to believe him, afraid to believe him. "What do you want?"

"You," he said evenly. "I want you, Rachel."

The breath stalled in her lungs. Rachel squeezed her eyes shut, striving to keep her emotions in check.

As the code came across the loudspeaker for her to report to the E.R., Rachel snapped her eyes open. "I have to go," she told him, and started for the door suddenly glad for an excuse to escape. She needed time to think, time to figure out what she was going to do. The last thing she wanted was to read more into Mac's words than he meant.

"What time do you get off?" he asked, following on her heels as she exited the employees' lounge.

"Not until four o'clock." She started toward the elevators with Mac matching her steps.

"I'll pick you up."

"No!" Rachel swallowed and, lowering her voice, said, "I...I have plans."

He didn't like it. She could see it in the set of his jaw, the way his eyes narrowed. "All right. When?"

"Tonight," she said, praying Chloe would be able to watch P.J. for a few extra hours that evening. Mac followed her into the elevator and the doors slid shut, locking them in the confined space alone.

"What time?" he asked, looming over her so tall, so strong, so fierce. She'd almost forgotten how devastating Mac McKenna could be. No, that wasn't true. She hadn't forgotten. She'd simply tried her best to forget.

"Rach, what time?"

"Seven o'clock. Irene's in the French Quarter?" she suggested and immediately kicked herself mentally for choosing the restaurant they had frequented as a couple.

"Irene's is fine. I'll pick you up at say six-thirty?"

The doors of the elevator slid open. "I'll meet you there," Rachel told him, and hurried out before he could object.

She wasn't going to show, Mac conceded at half past eight that evening. He tossed back the last of his wine and motioned for the waiter.

"Another glass of merlot while you wait for your lady, Commander?"

"No thanks, Sergio," Mac replied, still amazed that the man who'd been a fixture at the Italian eatery two years ago, when he and Rachel had frequented the place, actually remembered him.

"Then perhaps you will allow Sergio to bring you a

small appetizer, just a little something to tide you over until the lady arrives.''

''Thanks. I appreciate the offer, but I'll just take the check.''

''But your plans for dinner…'' he objected.

''Are off. It doesn't look like the lady's going to make it.''

''Ah, a pity,'' the older man said with a frown that formed a crease between his brows that extended to his receding hairline. He placed the black leather folio with the bill on top of the table. ''I am sorry.''

''Yeah, me, too.'' After a quick glance at the check, Mac dropped a twenty inside—enough to cover the cost of the two glasses of wine he'd nursed while waiting for Rachel and a generous tip for the disappointed Sergio.

''Thank you, Commander,'' Sergio murmured as he picked up the folio. ''You and your lady will come to Irene's again soon and ask for Sergio, yes?''

''Sure,'' Mac replied.

But don't count on it, Mac added silently because he didn't hold out a lot of hope that he would be dining with Rachel at Irene's or anywhere else in the near future. Picking up his hat, Mac headed for the exit. Even if he hadn't completely blown things by showing up out of the blue at the hospital today, the chances of Rachel wanting to share so much as a cup of coffee with him were slim at best. While she hadn't thrown him out, she hadn't exactly welcomed him with open arms, either. Her crack about his reasons for coming to see her had gnawed at him all day. Was that how she remembered him? As some sort of stud who had used and discarded her? The idea that she might believe such a thing filled him with self-disgust. If she did believe him so callous, she'd probably only agreed to meet him in the first place in order to get rid of him.

Not that he blamed her, Mac conceded as he stepped outside into the chilled night air. If whatever she'd once felt for him had been replaced with resentment, he supposed he deserved it. And probably a lot more. To say he'd handled things badly two years ago when he'd left was an understatement. He'd flat-out bungled it, he admitted. The truth was he hadn't wanted to leave her, and that fact alone had left him scared spitless.

Lost in thought, he scarcely registered that the weather, unpredictable as always, had gone from a balmy breeze to a brisk November wind. Unfazed by the sharp bite of cold air that met him when he turned the corner, Mac walked down the dimly lit street. As a SEAL, he'd been trained to master his body's reaction to swift temperature changes, be it Arctic winds or desert heat. What he hadn't been trained for was this sense of…uselessness.

Picking up his pace, Mac continued determinedly, striding headfirst into the cold gusts that swept through the narrow French Quarter streets. He walked faster, needing to burn up some of the restlessness churning inside him—a restlessness that had begun long before the minefield explosion that had damaged his hearing and had only worsened since he'd been placed on medical leave. But as he walked the historic streets of the city, Mac's thoughts kept turning to the last time he'd walked these same streets. It had been hot then. Hot and humid as only New Orleans in September could be. And he'd been with Rachel.

He cringed at the memory of her face when he'd told her he was leaving and that she should forget him. As long as he lived, he'd never be able to erase the image of her brave but tremulous smile, of seeing the light go out of her eyes. He'd handled the situation with all the finesse of a bull in a china shop. The fact that he'd been in over his head and had been shaken by how important she had become to him, to where those feelings for her would lead him, didn't excuse his actions.

Nor did it excuse the fact that he'd hurt her. Deeply, he suspected—despite the fact that there had been no tears, no accusations, no pleas for him to change his mind. But he'd known he had hurt her just the same. He'd seen the hurt in those sad gray eyes when he'd told her a clean break was best. He'd heard the hurt in her voice when she'd told him that she understood. And he'd tasted the hurt when she'd kissed him goodbye and wished him well.

And now here he was more than two years later showing up to ask her...

To ask her what, McKenna? To give you a second chance?

Hell, he didn't know what he wanted to ask her or even how much he wanted to tell her. Maybe it was just as well that she had stood him up tonight. He would have probably made a fool of himself if she had come. His thoughts turned inward, Mac barely noticed the sidewalk musicians as he crossed the street and continued down to the next block. As a SEAL he hadn't been able to offer Rachel any future. No way would he have asked her to commit herself to him knowing that the very nature of his job meant he might not make it back from one mission to the next. He'd learned firsthand the damage that kind of selfishness could cause. But now...

Now what, McKenna? What kind of future could he offer her now? Why should Rachel settle for a man who was damaged goods. Not even the SEALs wanted him anymore.

Anger and frustration stormed inside him as he recalled the conversation with his captain three days ago....

"Damn it, Mac, this sucks. But you know as well as I do that a SEAL's got to be physically 100 percent. Loss of hearing, even in just one ear..." Captain Mike Rossi *rammed a fist through his hair. He looked Mac square in the eye. "I'm sorry, kid. I really am. But I can't risk the safety of the rest of the team."*

Standing at attention, his back ramrod straight, Mac felt as though he'd just been plowed down by a tank. It didn't matter that he'd known it was coming. He'd expected to be cut loose from the team for nearly two months now, ever since the explosion in the raid on that embassy had left the hearing in his right ear diminished. Yet even anticipating the inevitable didn't lessen the impact of the blow when it came. "I understand, Captain."

"You've got a lot of leave coming. Take it, Mac. Go to New Orleans. Talk to the specialists at the base hospital there. I understand they're doing some great things. Find out all you can about that new surgical procedure and then decide if it's worth the risk or not."

"I've already decided to have the surgery, sir."

The captain frowned. "You should check it out first. Weigh all the risks before you make any decision. Forty percent hearing is better than none."

"Forty percent isn't good enough to be a SEAL, sir."

"Being a SEAL isn't everything."

"It is for me, sir." Which was the truth. For him being a SEAL wasn't just *what* he was or did, it was *who* he was. And if he could no longer be a SEAL, he was...he was no one.

The captain's frown deepened. "This isn't something you should make a snap decision about, Mac."

"I know. And I've given it a lot of thought, Captain. I want to have the surgery."

"Check it out first, SEAL. That's an order. Afterward if you still want to go through with it, it's your choice. But if I were you, I'd think long and hard before I make any decision. And while you're thinking, it wouldn't hurt to look up that lady friend of yours who lives there and maybe see how she feels about it."

Mac had hoped that the captain's failure to comment on him getting dog-faced when he'd broken things off with Rachel two years ago and his lack of interest in any woman since had gone unnoticed. He should have realized that Eagle Eye Mike Rossi never missed a thing when it came to the members of his SEAL team. "I...we ended things the last time I was in New Orleans. Things weren't that serious between us." *Or rather Mac had decided to end things because they were getting too serious, he admitted in silence.*

Rossi gave him a knowing look. "Too bad. It might make a difference in your decision if she were still in the picture."

Rachel wasn't in the picture anymore, Mac reminded himself. Yet, here he was anyway because he hadn't been able to stay away from her. Just as he hadn't been able to forget her, regardless of how many missions he went on or how many willing women he could have had in his bed since he'd left her.

And now that he'd seen her again, he was no closer to banishing Rachel from his thoughts than he had been when he'd walked out of her life two years ago. If anything, he wanted her even more.

So what are you going to do about it?

Dammit, he was still a SEAL, Mac reminded himself. A member of the U.S. military's fiercest, bravest and smartest band of warriors. A SEAL didn't walk away from a battle because the odds were stacked against him. A SEAL found a way to even the odds and win.

"Hey, sailor," a sidewalk barker standing outside one of the nightclubs called out in that unmistakable drawl that marked him as a New Orleanian. Opening the door a fraction, the giant of a man offered Mac a glimpse of a long-limbed woman dancing onstage to the seductive wail of a sax. "Why don't you come on in out of the cold, my man? Lovely Lola's next show is about to start any minute. You have my word," he said with a smile that glinted with gold. "Lola's act will warm you right up and make you glad you're a man."

"Thanks, pal," Mac said with an answering grin. "But there's another lady I've got to see."

Rachel didn't see him at first—not until after she had climbed the stairs and deactivated the alarm to the house. Bone tired from a day that had started with the shock of Mac showing up at the hospital and ended with her pulling an extra stint in the E.R., she'd driven home on automatic pilot. Tomorrow she would worry about Mac, she promised herself. Tomorrow she would sort out how she felt about the things he'd said to her, and she would figure out how to break the news to him about P.J.

But right now…right now all she wanted to do was crawl into her bed and sleep. Stifling a yawn, she reached into her purse for the house key when a movement from the far end of the veranda caught her eye.

Rachel froze. The weariness of a moment ago dissolved in a heartbeat. Fear-induced adrenaline took its place. Suddenly she realized how vulnerable she was, standing alone in the darkness, illuminated by the glow of the porch lamp Chloe had left on for her. Since it was long past midnight, the street was quiet save for the wind whistling through the oaks. No lights burned in her neighbor's homes. No cars made their way down the silent street. She was alone and even if she screamed for help, no one was likely to come to her aid in time.

Quickly she gauged her chances of getting the door unlocked and safely inside before he realized she'd spotted him. She couldn't risk it, she decided. Not with P.J. asleep in the house. Seconds ticked by in which fear knotted like an icy fist in her stomach. She tried to recall the techniques she'd learned in that self-defense class and drew a blank.

She had to do something! Beads of perspiration dampened her brow despite the cold temperatures. Fighting back the panic that threatened, she told herself to think. Then she remembered—the mace! She had a can of mace in her purse. Her heart thundering in her ears, Rachel closed her fingers around the metal cylinder. "Who's there?" she demanded in a voice that sounded surprisingly strong given the fact that her legs felt like jelly.

Keeping her eyes trained on the corner where she'd detected the movement, Rachel lifted the can like a gun and aimed. "I know you're there. So you might as well come out."

Suddenly a hand shot out from behind her, disarming her so quickly that her finger was still poised to shoot. At the same time another hand clamped over her mouth midscream, and she felt herself being pulled back against a very hard, very strong, very male body.

"Rach, it's me."

With the metallic taste of fear in her mouth and her heart beating frantically, his words failed to register. She kicked at his legs. She jabbed her elbow into his midsection. Panicked, she wished for a pair of killer stilettos as she lifted her foot and did a karate-style back kick to his shin. She barely heard her captor's grunt as stars exploded in front of her eyes and pain ricocheted up her leg.

"Rach, cut it out! It's me," he repeated. "It's Mac."

Rachel stilled. "Mac?" she mumbled the name against the hand covering her mouth.

"Yeah," he told her as he removed his hand from over her mouth.

Suddenly weak with relief, Rachel whooshed out a breath. It was Mac. Not a mugger. Not a burglar. It was Mac. And, she realized in the next breath, it was Mac who had just scared her silly.

Slowly he loosened the arm anchored around her waist. "I'm sorry. I didn't mean to frighten you."

Relief swiftly gave way to anger, and Rachel whirled around to face him. "Frighten me? You scared me half to death," she accused, her voice shaking with fury. "What are you doing here slinking around in the dark? And how did you find out where I live?"

"I wasn't slinking around. I was waiting for you. Since you never made it to the restaurant, I came by hoping we could talk. And as for finding out where you live, I'm a SEAL, Rach," he said crisply. "Finding you wasn't hard."

Her breath was still coming fast, but already the edge of her anger was cooling. "I-I'm sorry about dinner. But you still should have said something. You should have at least let me know you were there."

"I started to, but when I saw how tired you looked, I decided tonight wasn't a good time. I was waiting to make sure you got inside safely before I left. Then I was going to call you in the morning and see about rescheduling our date."

"It wasn't a date," Rachel corrected. "It was dinner between...between acquaintances."

Mac snorted. "We were a bit more than acquaintances."

Deciding it best to ignore that remark, Rachel explained, "I got tied up at the hospital. That's why I didn't meet you at the restaurant. There was an accident. A bus filled with high school kids on their way to a football game was rear-ended by an eighteen-wheeler."

"I heard. Was it bad?"

"Not really. Mostly bumps and bruises. A few stitches, a couple of sprains and one broken ankle." Suddenly, standing alone in the dim porch light with Mac felt too intimate. It reminded Rachel of other nights when they had stood in the moonlight and she'd recounted the events of her day for him. Slamming the door shut on her memories, she tucked her hands into the pockets of her coat. "Anyway, by the time I got a break and was able to call the restaurant, you'd already left. I didn't know how else to contact you."

"It's all right," Mac told her, the ghost of a smile on his lips. He ran his thumb along her jaw in a gesture that was tender, loving...like the look in his eyes.

No, she wouldn't do that to herself again, Rachel vowed, and turned her face away from his touch. But not before she caught the flare of emotion in his eyes. For a second she almost believed that she had hurt Mac. Just as quickly, Rachel dismissed the notion. More likely she'd been right earlier today, and she had simply dashed Mac's hopes for a quick reunion while he was in town. Swallowing hard, she reminded herself of what a mistake their relationship had been the first time. It was a mistake she had no intention of repeating. "All the same I'm sorry about standing you up."

"Quit apologizing, Rachel. Your roommate already explained about the flu hitting the hospital's staff and how you had to pull an extra shift in the E.R."

"My roommate?"

"Chloe."

Rachel sucked in a breath. "You talked to Chloe?"

"Yeah. When I came over to find out why you didn't show up at the restaurant, she answered the door and told me what happened."

"I see," Rachel murmured. She *had* called Chloe to let her know she'd be even later than she'd first thought tonight. And then she had called the restaurant for Mac.

"I liked her. She seems really nice."

"She is," Rachel informed him. Chloe Chancellor *was* nice. And she was so much more than a roommate. She was also Rachel's friend. It had been Chloe who had comforted her during those first lonely weeks after Mac had left. It had been Chloe who had bullied her into taking care of herself when she'd first discovered she was pregnant. It had been Chloe who had insisted she hated living in the big, old house alone and had convinced her to get out of her tiny apartment and move in with her so that P.J. would have a real home.

And it had been Chloe who had insisted she was wasting her time by dating Alex. According to Chloe, who had known Alex Jenkins since they were kids, the good doctor had grown up to be a major stuffed shirt who wanted what he perceived to be a perfect wife. A position that, according to Chloe again, Rachel appeared to fit perfectly. But ever the romantic, Chloe believed marriages should be entered into for one reason only—love. And, of course, Chloe had been enthralled by the tale of her affair with Mac and had long since made up her mind that Mac was the only man Rachel would ever love. She certainly prayed her friend was wrong, Rachel thought.

"She's a very gifted artist."

Rachel jerked her attention back to Mac. "Chloe invited you inside?"

"She practically insisted when I told her who I was. Anyway, I happened to notice the artwork. She seemed a little surprised that I thought they were good. Then she admitted they were hers and I got her to point out a few of the others she'd done. Like I said, she's very talented."

"I know she is." It was Chloe, who for all her bravado, doubted her own talent.

"She's agreed to sell me one of the small oils for my mother."

"Sounds like you two hit it off," Rachel said with dismay.

Mac grinned at that. "My guess is the uniform had something to do with it. That, and the fact that she apparently knew who I was. I take it you told her about us."

"I may have mentioned your name to her in passing," Rachel replied, knowing as she said the words what a whopper she was telling. Chloe had listened to her sob her heart out far more times that she cared to remember after Mac had left. And she had been the one in the delivery room with her when she'd borne Mac's son. Thoughts of their son had her nerves—already wound tight as a spring—growing even more strained. Rachel held her breath and waited for Mac to mention P.J.

The smile disappeared from his lips. "Then I guess I'm lucky she didn't slam the door in my face."

"Why would she do that?"

"Come on, Rach. I can't imagine you would have

many nice things to say about me, considering how badly
I handled things before I left.''

Rachel met his somber gaze. ''Then you'd be wrong,
Mac.'' No matter how things had ended between them
or how deeply he had hurt her, she would always be
grateful to him for giving her P.J.

''Rach,'' Mac said her name like a prayer as he moved
in, cupped her shoulders. ''If only you knew how many
times I—''

The lights flickered on inside and after a quick snick
of locks, the door opened to reveal a sleepy-eyed Chloe
clutching her big fluffy robe around her. ''Are you guys
deliberately trying to catch pneumonia? It's freezing out
there.''

''Sorry, ma'am. I didn't mean to wake you,'' Mac told
her.

''You didn't. The little monster did.''

Rachel stiffened at her friend's words, and the frown
on Mac's face set her nerves to racing again. ''I'd better
go,'' she told him, hoping to hurry him along. ''I'll talk
to you in the morning.''

Ignoring her dismissal, Mac kept his focus on Chloe.
''Little monster?'' he repeated, a determined expression
on his face.

''P.J.,'' Chloe offered with a yawn.

''P.J.?''

As if on cue, P.J. let out a squeal guaranteed to wake
the dead. And just as she knew he would, he came wad-
dling over to the door on his little chubby legs, his arms
outstretched. ''Mama,'' he said, one of the few words in
his limited baby vocabulary that anyone could understand.

''You have a son?'' Mac asked Chloe.

Seeing no hope for postponing the truth, Rachel reached for her son. Holding him in her arms, she turned back to face Mac. "He's not Chloe's son, Mac. He's mine."

Two

"*Yours*?" Mac repeated, feeling as though he'd been sucker punched.

Rachel hiked up her chin. "That's right," she told him. "*Mine*."

Still reeling from the shock of discovering Rachel had a child, Mac looked from her to the dark-haired boy in her arms and back again. Rachel's son and his, Mac realized as he stared into eyes identical to his own.

He had a son. A son!

A son he'd known nothing about.

Suddenly shock gave way to temper as the reality of the situation hit him. He kept his eyes trained on Rachel's face. And even though he already suspected he knew the answer he asked her, anyway, "How old is he?"

When Rachel remained silent, he asked again. "How old is he, Rachel?"

"He's eighteen months," Chloe offered, and earned a scowl from Rachel.

He didn't have to be a math wizard to figure out that Rachel had been about four weeks pregnant when he had left New Orleans. Had she known about the baby and chosen not to tell him? Or had she found out later and decided he didn't deserve to know that he was going to be a father?

Either situation left a foul taste in his mouth and did nothing to ease his anger with Rachel or with himself. Doing his best to control the emotions slamming through him, Mac said, "Which means I'm his father."

"Of course you're his father," Chloe told him as she moved beside Rachel and placed a protective hand on her shoulder. She looked him up and down, narrowed her eyes. "All you have to do is look at him to see that. Or do you need proof?"

Rachel groaned.

"No, ma'am. I don't need proof. He's my son," Mac announced, daring Rachel to deny it.

She didn't. She simply hugged the squirming tike to her.

"Down," the little boy insisted.

"No, P.J. It's time—"

"May I?" Mac asked. Taking a step forward, he held out his arms. When Rachel hesitated, he added, "You don't have to worry that I'll drop him. I have a couple of nieces and nephews. I'll be careful."

Rachel said nothing. She simply handed him the baby.

"Hey, big guy," Mac managed to say past the lump in his throat. He stared at this miniature version of himself, recognizing the strong McKenna chin, the eyes so like his own. The nose was Rachel's, though, he thought. So was the mouth. But there was no question that he was a McKenna. His son. His son, Mac repeated silently, rocked again by the realization that he and Rachel had created a child. When the boy reached for the hat Mac had forgotten was clutched in his fist, Mac laughed and gave it to him. "Hey, you're a strong fellow, aren't you?"

"He's also stubborn," Rachel offered. "No, no, P.J.," she told him, and rescued the hat before the little guy could chomp down on it.

"What's P.J. stand for?" he asked.

"Peter James."

Surprised, Mac met Rachel's gaze. "You gave him my name?"

"Actually I gave him our father's names. I remembered you saying you were named after your father. And my dad's name is James. I hadn't planned to give him a nickname, but somehow, the initials seemed to fit him."

Sort of the way the name Mac had always fitted him better than the names Peter or junior, Mac thought. "It happens that way sometimes," Mac offered and noted the way P.J. was eyeing his medals. "It's all right, P.J. You can touch them," Mac encouraged, and earned a grin that warmed him down to his toes.

"That might not be such a good idea. I'm afraid that he's at that stage where everything goes into his mouth," Rachel began, but P.J. was already trying to sample one of the medals. "No, no, P.J. No eat," Rachel corrected.

"Your mom's right, buddy. Trust me. They look a lot better than they taste." Reluctantly he started to hand him off to Rachel. P.J. had other ideas. Clinging to the medal, he began to wail in protest.

"Come on, sweetie," Rachel cooed.

Those big, fat tears nearly did him in. "Hey, it's okay," Mac said, and gave serious consideration to rip-ping off his shirt and giving it to the little fellow. "Why don't I just—"

Rachel leveled him with a look, and he fell silent as she pried the chubby little fingers free from his shirtfront. "There, there now. It's all right, angel," she murmured.

"Why don't I take him inside and give him a snack?" Chloe offered. "I'm sure you guys have things to discuss."

"Thanks, Chlo," Rachel said, and relinquished the sniffling P.J. to the other woman.

"Come on, handsome. What do you say? Aunt Chloe is in the mood for cookies. Want to help me find some?"

"Tookie?" the tear-eyed tike repeated.

"That's right," Chloe told him, and disappeared inside the house.

Mac's heart was still trying to recover from the impact of those tears rolling down P.J.'s cheeks when Rachel said, "He'll be fine, Mac. He's a baby, and babies cry."

"Yeah, I know. It's just that he was crying so hard."

"That's because the tears work all too well. He has a very strong will and doesn't like being told no. Unfortunately, I don't use the word often enough. And neither does Chloe."

"Yeah. Well, it's easy to see why. He's a cute kid."

"I certainly think so."

And he's my son.

His son and Rachel's. The reality of that fact hit him again.

The realization excited him.

It scared the hell out of him.

And it infuriated him to realize that he had missed the first year and a half of his son's life. He shifted his gaze from the doorway, where P.J. had disappeared with Chloe, back to Rachel. She was tired. Even in the dim light on the veranda, he could see the shadows beneath her eyes. Strands of honey-colored hair had worked free of the braid she wore and now framed her face. A face that was far too pale. Yet seeing her exhausted like this only added to his frustration because he realized that not only had she had to support herself, but their son as well, without any help from him. "Why didn't you tell me about him, Rachel? Didn't you think I deserved to know?"

"Of course," she answered. "And I wanted to tell you. I probably sat down to write you a hundred times, but I didn't know where you were."

"You could have reached me through Delta Team Six."

"I know. And I was going to…"

"Then why didn't you?"

"Because I didn't know *how* to tell you," she said, some of the strain and weariness coming through in her voice. A gust of wind whipped across the veranda, and she huddled deeper into the navy-blue jacket she wore.

Mac immediately stepped in front of her to block the wind. "You're shivering. Maybe we should go inside where—"

"No," she shot back. "I'm fine. Really. I'd rather…I'd rather we talked out here."

Though a part of him could understand her not wanting him in her home after the way he'd ended things between them, the rejection stung all the same. Probably because there had been a time when Rachel had eagerly welcomed him into the tiny apartment that had been her home, he reasoned. Of course, they had been lovers at the time, and she had believed herself to be in love with him.

As eager as he was for answers, it was obvious she

was exhausted. "Maybe you should get some rest, and I'll come back in the morning."

"No," Rachel snapped. "I'd just as soon answer your questions now."

Mac hesitated a moment. "Then you'd better sit down before you fall down." He motioned to the old-fashioned porch swing where he'd sat earlier to wait for her. "You're dead on your feet."

"I'm just tired. It's been a long day."

Mac recognized how she avoided touching him. Still, it didn't stop him from noticing the way her nurse's uniform rode up when she sat down or her efforts to tug the hem down toward her knees. Mac couldn't help remembering other evenings when she'd been pleased to see him waiting for her at the end of a long day. Or how quickly her fatigue melted beneath his kisses. They would barely make it inside the apartment before they'd be reaching for each other—hot, hungry, insatiable.

"I suppose you're wondering how this could have happened," Rachel began, looking everywhere but at him.

"If by 'this' you're referring to your getting pregnant, I have a pretty good idea. I was there remember? And I haven't forgotten anything about the time we spent together." Which was true. He hadn't been able to forget Rachel—despite his best efforts to do so.

"I was talking about the fact that we always used protection."

"Darling, we both know there's only one form of birth control that's guaranteed. Abstinence—which is something we didn't come anywhere close to exercising." Quite the contrary, Mac thought. During the month they had been together they had made love countless times, never seeming to be able to get enough of each other. And there had been one particularly steamy afternoon in

late August just before a rainstorm had flooded the city.
The desire between them had escalated along with the
high temperatures that day until every touch, every
glance, every breath had fed the gnawing ache inside
them both. "It was that afternoon of the big rainstorm,
wasn't it? The one that caused a power outage in the
city."

As though it were only yesterday, the images came
rushing back to Mac....

*"The snowballs were a great idea," he had told Ra-
chel as they'd strolled lazily down the sidewalk in the
unrelenting heat. Waves of heat shimmered from the
paved street, and Mac swallowed another mouthful of the
chocolate-and-cream-flavored ice. Despite the fact that it
was already past six in the evening and thunder rumbled
in the distance, the sun continued to beat down upon
them.*

*They turned the corner onto the street that led to her
apartment, and Rachel gasped at the rush of hot air. "I
can barely breathe," she complained. "Why aren't you
withering, too?"*

*Mac chuckled. "SEAL training, darling," he told her
and pitched his empty paper cup into the trash bin while
they waited for the traffic light to change so they could
cross the street. "You don't know the meaning of hot
until you've spent a week baking out in the desert."*

*"I'll take your word for it," she said dryly. Scooping
a few fingers of the ice-only snowball she'd opted for
from her cup, she began bathing her neck and collarbone
with the swiftly melting ice shavings.*

*Mac's mouth went dry at the sight of the water sliding
down her throat, past the open neck of her prim uniform
and disappearing between her breasts. It didn't matter
that they had made love less than two hours ago when*

she'd returned from work, his body responded immediately.

Rachel stilled. "Mac," she admonished, her voice thready. She clutched the cup to her chest.

Removing the cup from her hand, he grazed the side of her breast with his fingers. Desire shot through him like a missile as he watched the answering flare of hunger in her gray eyes. He tossed the cup into the trash bin. "Come on," he all but growled the command. Grabbing her hand, they raced down the long block toward her apartment. And while an observer might have attributed their mad dash to the fat drops of rain that began to pepper the city like bullets, he and Rachel both knew the urgency had nothing to do with the weather and everything to do with their fierce need for each other.

They rushed up the stairs. Rachel's hand trembled, and she dropped the key. Mac scooped it up. He slammed the key into the lock. And when the door opened, he ushered Rachel inside. The door had barely closed when Rachel reached for him.

"This is insane," she told him.

"Yeah," Mac agreed on a groan as she fumbled with the buttons of his shirt. When she brushed her hand down the front of his jeans, he thought he'd die right then and there. Dropping the keys to the floor, he caught Rachel's questing fingers. "Darling, you've got to slow down."

"I don't want to slow down," she told him and pressed her lips against his neck.

Mac switched positions so that she was the one caged against the door. With her wrists imprisoned in his fist, he lifted them over her head. His body throbbed at the anticipation and excitement in her eyes. He dipped his head, heard her moan as he used his mouth to follow the damp trail left by the ice and rain. With teeth and tongue and lips, he sampled her neck, her collarbone. Using his free hand, he began unbuttoning the front of her uniform. When he reached the snap at the front of her bra, he twisted it open and tasted her flesh.

"Mac," she whispered urgently, struggling to free her wrists.

He circled first one nipple, then the other with his tongue. And when he took one rosy crest into his mouth, she moaned again and pulled her hands free. She grabbed his face, pulled his mouth up to hers.

And she kissed him deep, her tongue sparring with his, her never-still fingers raced over him. When she reached for his belt and fought with the snap of his jeans, Mac tore his mouth free. "Rachel," he gasped her name. Realizing how close to the edge he was, he sucked air into his lungs. "Darling, I'm about ten steps ahead of you," he explained. "You need to give me a minute to slow down so you can catch up with me."

She looked up at him out of eyes hot with desire. "I've got news for you, Lieutenant Commander," she said, leveling him with a smile that was pure sin. She wiggled her fingers free and reached for the tab of his zipper. "You're the one who has to catch up with me."

Mac lost it. Any hope he had of reining in his own hunger went up in smoke. The small part of his brain that still functioned registered the lightning flash that illuminated the draped windows, the sound of rain pounding the rooftop, the squeals and slap of footsteps as people caught in the rain hurried past the door outside. But nature's fireworks were no match for the fire in his blood.

He eased his palms from her waist to her hips, continued down until he reached the hem of her skirt. Then he slid his hands up her legs, beneath the edge of her panties, cupped her moist heat. When Rachel whimpered, pressed herself against him, Mac quickly discarded the scrap of lace. He tested her with his fingers.

"Mac," she cried out. "Hurry."

"In my pocket. Protection," he told her.

And right there against her front door—with the crash of thunder ringing in his ears and the rain beating down on the roof, she wrapped those long, smooth legs of hers around his waist and he thrust into her.

Rachel trembled, clutched at him as he began to move inside her fast, faster and faster still. And when the first climax hit her, she shuddered in his arms and cried out, "I love you, Mac. I love you."

Emotion had ripped through him at her declaration, swelled in his chest as she'd clung to him, and he'd thrust deeply again and again. And just as his own release had fired through him and he'd followed her over the edge into the storm, the condom had broken.

Rachel could feel the tide of color climb up her cheeks. She remembered all too clearly the night Mac was referring to. Even now, she had trouble reconciling the person she knew herself to be with her so out-of-character behavior with Mac that summer. Somehow during those wild weeks they had been together, falling in love with Mac had transformed her from the shy, conservative minister's daughter into some bold, wanton woman she didn't recognize. A woman who had shamelessly urged her lover to make love with her standing up inside the front door of her apartment. One look at Mac's face and she knew he was remembering, too.

"When the condom broke. That's when it happened. That's when you got pregnant, isn't it?"

"Probably," she said, averting her gaze because just the memory still had the power to make her ache. She had loved him and had foolishly believed that Mac couldn't possibly make love to her as he had and not feel the same way. And she'd been proven dead wrong. "Based on when P.J. was born, it was around that time."

"Rach, that day when I came to say goodbye," Mac began, his voice low, soft, as though it were difficult for him to speak. "Did you...did you know that you were pregnant?"

"No," she whispered, surprised by the emotion swimming in his eyes. "I mean I knew I was late," she explained. "But I'd been late before. It wasn't until about a month after you'd left that I started getting sick in the morning and realized I might be pregnant. So I made an appointment with my doctor, and he confirmed it."

"You shouldn't have had to go through that alone," he said, his expression as somber as his voice. "I'm sorry."

"I wasn't alone. I had Chloe. And my parents. They were wonderful about everything. They helped me."

"But they shouldn't have had to. It...you and P.J. were my responsibility," he argued. "If only you'd contacted my unit, my CO would have gotten word to me."

"I told you I thought about it, but in the end I decided against it. There was nothing you could have done."

"I could have been here for you," Mac insisted.

"How? You were God knows where doing your Navy SEAL thing, remember?"

"I would have gotten an emergency leave or something. I would have come back, been here for you," he told her, pacing as he spoke. "You didn't get pregnant by yourself. You were my responsibility, and I honor my responsibilities."

"By doing what? Offering to marry me?"

He stopped cold at the question. His fist stilled in his hair. "Yes," he told her, his eyes seeking hers.

But Rachel hadn't missed the slight hesitation. And it nearly broke her heart. He looked so brave, so strong, and she didn't doubt for a second that Mac meant it. He would have offered to marry her—for the baby's sake. Which was the reason she hadn't contacted him. She'd been so deeply in love with him at the time that she might have been tempted to accept his offer. And had she done so, it would have ruined both their lives. "It would never have worked, Mac."

"You don't know that."

"Yes, I do. And so do you. You said yourself that being a SEAL is who and what you are, that there isn't room in your life for anything or anyone else. A wife and baby would never have fit in with your plans, Mac. That's why you told me that I should get on with my life and forget you. That's what I've done. That's what we've both done. We've moved on with our lives."

"But that was before I knew about P.J."

"P.J. is my responsibility," she told him.

"He's my son. That makes him my responsibility, too."

Worry began to stir inside Rachel as she noted the determined expression on his face. She rubbed her arms against the chill that had nothing to do with the November temperature and everything to do with the very real threat of Mac coming back into her life. Even worse was the idea that he might insist on being a part of P.J.'s life. Then what would she do?

"P.J. is as much my responsibility as he is yours. I'm sorry you've had to shoulder that responsibility alone until now. But that's all going to change. I intend to do my part by—"

"Stop it," she said. Unable to sit still, she stood and walked to the end of the veranda.

"Rachel?"

She spun around, taken aback to find Mac so close. He'd always had that ability to move without making a sound. She moved past him, needing distance and a chance to marshal her thoughts.

"I'd think you'd be happy to have someone share the responsibility of P.J. with. It can't have been easy, shouldering everything by yourself. Now that I know, I—"

"Stop it," she cried out and spun around. "Don't you understand? I'm letting you off the hook here. I'm telling you there's no reason for you to feel guilty or responsible or anything else you might be feeling because our...our fling resulted in my getting pregnant. I may not have planned to have a baby, but I wanted him from the moment I found out he was growing inside me."

She bit down on her bottom lip, swallowed past the lump forming in her throat before lifting her gaze to meet his again. "Go back to your SEAL team, Mac. Ask your CO to send you off on some mission a million miles from New Orleans and forget about me. Forget you ever met me, that you ever found out about P.J. We don't need you. We're doing just fine without you."

"Well, hell, darling," he said, his voice mocking. "There's no need to soft pedal your opinion of me. You just go right ahead and give it to me straight. I can take it."

Rachel winced. Despite his glib comeback, she'd caught that flash of hurt in his eyes. And it made her feel lower than the belly of a snake. "I'm sorry. I'm not trying to be cruel. I'm simply trying to be honest with you. We both know that marriage and fatherhood were never in your plans. You made it clear to me two years ago that being a SEAL comes first for you, that there isn't room for anyone or anything else in your life. All I'm trying to tell you is that I understand. So you don't have to worry about me or about P.J. or that I'll try to make any demands on you—financially or…or otherwise. I love P.J. And I can support him and provide him with everything he needs.''

''But that's where you're wrong, darling. And while I don't doubt that you're the best mother in the world, there is one thing that you can't give him.''

Although she suspected she knew what he was going to say, she asked the question, anyway. ''What?''

''His father.''

''If you're worried he's lacking a father figure in his life, you're wrong. My dad adores P.J. He and my mother drive in from Mississippi every few weeks to see him. Or we drive to the coast to see them.''

''That's good to hear. Real good. I mean that. I never knew my own grandparents, and I would have liked to. It think it's important for a kid to establish a relationship with his grandparents, and I'm glad to know that P.J. has your folks. But as nice as that is, it's not enough.''

''But—''

''I'm P.J.'s father. Maybe I'm not the man you'd have chosen to be his dad. But it's a bit late for you to have much say in the matter. That afternoon you made love with me in your hallway and created P.J. pretty much took away your options. While I'll be the first one to admit that I'm no prize, I'm what you're stuck with. P.J.'s my son, and I intend to be a father to him. A real father—not just the man who got his mother pregnant.''

Still reeling from Mac's words, Rachel whipped her gaze to the doorway at the sound of a throat being cleared. She nearly groaned at the sight of Chloe leaning against the door with a speculative look in her eyes and a smug grin on her lips. She only prayed that her friend hadn't overheard what Mac had said.

"I'm sorry to interrupt," Chloe began, and directed a dazzling smile in Mac's direction. "Especially when it sounds as though the conversation was getting interesting."

Rachel sighed. So much for praying, she thought. "Did you need something, Chloe?"

"Not me. P.J. He's all tucked in again, but he insists that he can't go to sleep unless his mommy kisses him and his teddy good-night."

"I'm sorry, Mac. I have to go," Rachel said, and although she knew she would only be postponing things, she was relieved to have an excuse to end the conversation. Otherwise, she might do something foolish—like allow herself to think that he was right.

He wasn't, of course. She knew it, even if he didn't.

"Would you mind if I come inside and say good-night to him, too?"

The yearning in his blue eyes was so intense that for a moment Rachel felt herself weakening. Then she thought of P.J., of how difficult it would be for him to have Mac suddenly come into his life today and then be gone the next. "I don't think that's a good idea."

"Rachel," Chloe hissed in objection.

"It's late," Rachel said, ignoring her friend. "Seeing you again will only excite P.J. and make it that much more difficult for him to go to sleep," she explained. Which was all true Rachel reasoned. But it didn't stop her from feeling a stab of guilt at the disappointment on Mac's face.

"Sure. I understand," Mac told her.

"I...I need to go," she said, feeling like a first-class witch. "Goodbye, Mac."

"Not goodbye, Rachel. Good night." He tipped his head in Chloe's direction. "Ma'am, it's been a pleasure."

"Same here, Commander. Don't be a stranger."

Rachel shot her friend a look, but the redhead simply ignored her. So did Mac.

"Don't worry, ma'am, I don't intend to be," he said, and grinned. It wasn't the megawatt smile that she had found so hard to resist two years ago, Rachel acknowledged. But even that ghost of a smile was enough to make her stomach flutter—especially when he aimed it at her as he was doing now. "I'll be back. You can count on it."

Three

Mac punched the doorbell to Rachel's house again, setting off the soft, lazy chimes for a second time. She'd been dodging his calls long enough, Mac decided. Did she honestly think that by avoiding him he would simply go away and forget the fact that he had a son?

A son.

Mac scrubbed a hand down his face. Even after several days the realization that he had a child still shook him. Probably because he'd never planned on becoming a parent, Mac reasoned. Just as he hadn't planned on ever marrying. He'd ruled out both options a long time ago, determined to avoid that torment called love. After all, he'd seen what love could do to people—even good people like his parents.

From the time he was six years old, he could remember the sad look in his mother's eyes whenever the captain left for a mission. Then he'd come home and they'd be as happy as two peas in a pod—until his father was off again. He recalled seeing that lonely look in his mother's eyes, hearing her weeping in her room at night when she thought no one could hear her. Then after that last mission when the captain hadn't made it back, he'd watched all the joy go out of his mother. She'd been left a widow before she'd turned forty, and with three children to raise alone. Unlike his siblings at least he'd had his father for ten years. His brothers hardly remembered the captain at all.

He'd finally realized then how selfish his father's decision to remain a SEAL had been. It didn't change his determination to become a SEAL himself someday. Nothing could—not even his father's death. Being a SEAL was the only thing he'd ever wanted to do with his life, the only thing he'd ever planned to do. But he'd made up his mind—right then and there at the funeral that he would never be selfish like his father had been. Sometimes choices had to be made, should be made, he reasoned. And he had made his. He would never subject any woman to the kind of pain his mother had suffered, worrying, wondering, afraid the man she loved and lived for wouldn't make it back. If and when that time came for him, he didn't want anyone's tears on his head. He sure as hell didn't intend to leave behind any kids to grow up without a father the way his two younger brothers had been forced to do.

Maybe some SEALs felt they could have both—a career as a SEAL and a family. But the way he saw it there were too many risks involved, too many chances that things could go wrong. It was a risk he'd chosen not to take and had stood by his decision.

Until now.

Now everything had changed. Whether he'd planned

on it or not, he *was* a father. Which meant he had a responsibility. To P.J. To Rachel. No way did he intend to walk away from either of those responsibilities and pretend they didn't exist. He'd worked it all out in his head that night after leaving Rachel's. They would get married, be a real family. The truth was, he kind of liked the idea, he admitted. If he were going to marry anyone, there was no question in his mind that the one woman he would want for a wife would be Rachel. She'd been special—more special than he'd wanted her to be, which was one of the reasons he'd ended things as he had two years ago. And when it came to sexual compatibility, well there was no question that they were well matched. Yes, there was definitely an upside to marrying Rachel, he thought, envisioning how it would be to come home to her night after night, to have her share his home, his bed, his life.

And then there was P.J. Mac thought about the dark-haired bundle of energy, recalled the way the little boy had looked at him. Suddenly his chest tightened with pride and what he could only describe as a longing to be a good father to his son, to be there for him. To teach him how to ride a bike, to swim, to hit a baseball, to drive a car, to explain the mystery of girls. And he would do all those things for P.J., Mac promised himself. Because he intended to do the one thing his father had been too selfish to do for him. He would resign his commission.

Despite the cool morning temperatures, an icy sweat broke out across his brow as he thought of walking away from his SEAL team. But it wasn't like he had any options, Mac reminded himself. Even without the surprise of P.J., there was always the chance that he might have to leave the SEAL team, anyway. His visit with the doc-

tors and surgeons yesterday about his hearing problem
had pretty much confirmed everything he'd been told already. The surgery had a 45 percent success rate. If it
was successful, his hearing would be restored. If it
wasn't, he ran the risk of it being diminished further as
a result of the procedure. The way he saw it whether he
had the surgery or not was a moot point now, since he
had no intention of remaining with the SEALs—not
when he had a son and, with luck, a wife.

It was the wife part that was going to be tricky, Mac
admitted, and gave the doorbell another push. Rachel
hadn't been at all keen on the idea of marrying him the
other night. The truth was, the idea had caught him by
surprise, too. But now that he'd had time to think about
it, he knew it was the right thing to do. Surely Rachel
would see that, wouldn't she? She had to realize that they
owed P.J. a real home, one with both parents.

Mac frowned as he waited for Rachel to come to the
door, and wondered how she would feel about him once
he told her about the hearing loss and surgery. The
SEALs didn't want him unless he was whole. Would she
feel the same way? Unsettled, he jammed his hands into
the pocket of his slacks—and hit the square box with the
ring. Closing his fist around the box that contained the
engagement ring he'd purchased helped him to focus.
First things first, he reminded himself. The first thing he
had to do was convince Rachel that they should get married. Then he would deal with the rest of it. And with
that thought in mind, he leaned on the doorbell a third
time.

"I'm coming. I'm coming. Keep your shirt on," a
woman called out from somewhere inside the house.

Mac strained to listen, frustrated that he wasn't sure if
it was Rachel he'd heard or not. At what sounded like a

thump, followed by a muttered oath, Mac winced and knew for sure that it wasn't Rachel en route to the door. In the short time he'd spent with her, he'd quickly learned that swearing was not one of Rachel Grant's vices. Probably comes from having a minister for a father, he thought, and immediately sobered as he realized just how difficult having a baby without the benefit of marriage must have been for Rachel. It was one more thing he would have to make up to her.

After a series of snicks, a "damn, I broke my nail," the door opened and revealed an obviously disgruntled Chloe Chancellor clad in a celery-colored robe with bright pink flowers on it and clutching her bare foot. "Good Lord, Commander, what are you doing here in the middle of the night?"

"I...um, actually it's morning, ma'am," he said, suddenly realizing that maybe showing up at Rachel's doorstep at the crack of dawn to propose might not have been such a good idea after all.

"But it can't be morning already."

"Sorry, ma'am, but I'm afraid it is."

"Are you sure?"

She looked so genuinely disappointed that he almost wished he could tell her otherwise. "Positive, ma'am."

She looked past him and squinted up at the sky. "I suppose you're going to tell me that that little streak of light trying to break through those dark clouds is the sun?"

"Yes, ma'am, it is."

She groaned, leaned her head against the door. "What time is it?"

"Just past oh-six-hundred hours, ma'am."

She lifted her head, peered at him out of sleepy brown eyes. "Commander, let's get something straight. I'm not very good at deciphering Navy talk when I'm fully awake. I can promise you there's no way that stuff computes when I'm still half-asleep and haven't had my first cup of coffee."

"Sorry, ma'am. It's just past six o'clock."

"Six o'clock! In the a.m.?"

He nodded and had to bite back a grin at her horrified expression.

"No wonder I feel like I've been run over by a truck. I've only been asleep for three hours."

"I'm sorry, ma'am. I didn't mean to wake you," he said, kicking himself for not realizing that in his effort to corner Rachel before she could dodge him again he might intrude on Chloe.

"Forget it," she told him even as she stifled a yawn. "Rachel's always on my case about sleeping away the best part of the day. Maybe I'll give this morning stuff she's always raving about a try."

"Yes, ma'am. If you could just—"

"Come on in," she said, cutting him off as she pulled the door wider so that he could enter. "I'll put some coffee on."

Not wanting to intrude further, he remained outside on the veranda. "Thanks, but I don't want to put you to any trouble," he explained. All he wanted to do was speak to Rachel.

"It's no trouble. I told you, I haven't had my coffee yet. And if I'm going to give this morning stuff a try, I definitely need coffee," she informed him, then squealed as a gust of cold air whipped across the veranda to the door. "Good heavens, Commander, it's freezing out there and you're not even wearing a coat. You'd better get in here before you catch pneumonia or something."

"Honestly, ma'am, I'm fine. If you could just tell—"

"Oh for pity's sake," she said and, grabbing him by the arm, she all but dragged him inside and then shoved the door closed behind him. "Tell me, Commander. Are all you dolphin guys this stubborn?"

"SEALs, ma'am," he corrected even as she marched down the foyer.

"Seals, dolphins, whatever. I knew it was some kind of sea creature." She paused, looked back, and when she noted he hadn't moved, she propped her hands on her hips. "You coming?"

Seeing no option, Mac followed her to the kitchen, where he noted the white wooden cabinets, Formica countertops and cheery lemon and white curtains at the windows. He spied the high chair next to the breakfast table and once again felt a surge of emotion as he imagined P.J. sitting in it.

"If you ask me, the Navy should reconsider what they call you guys. Dolphins sounds a lot more attractive to me than seals," she told him as she set out mugs and spoons on the counter, then tapped her foot impatiently while the coffee brewed.

"Actually, the term SEAL stands for sea, air and land."

She gave him a blank look.

"Sea, air and land," he repeated. "We specialize in those type of operations and since the first letters spell out the word SEAL our unit of the Navy goes by the name SEAL."

"Commander, my guess is you've already figured out that I'm not what you'd call a morning person. Right?"

"Yes, ma'am."

"Then I'll make you a deal. I won't try to educate you on the various aspects of art. And in turn, you don't try to educate me about the Navy stuff. Do we have a deal?"

''We have a deal,'' Mac told her, his lips twitching at her serious expression. ''I really am sorry about waking you so early. I forget that you artistic types keep different hours. The truth is, I'll get out of your way now, if you could just tell Ra—''

''Commander,'' she said, holding up her hand. ''Let me explain something. When I said I wasn't a morning person, I meant I'm not much for conversation, either. So could we cut the chatter until I get my coffee, please?''

Mac fell silent and waited while she poured two cups of coffee...or rather one full cup of coffee and one half cup. She handed him the full one and motioned toward the sugar and cream. When he shook his head, she proceeded to pour what had to be five teaspoons of sugar and at least four ounces of cream into the other cup. After stirring the concoction, she lifted it to her lips, closed her eyes and drank deeply.

Mac watched in fascination, half expecting the woman to gag on the mixture. Instead she opened her eyes and sighed. ''I think I just might live after all,'' she murmured and gave him a smile. She took a seat at the breakfast table and patted the chair next to hers. ''Now come have a seat and tell me what has you on my doorstep at such an unholy hour of the day.''

''I need to see Rachel.''

''Ah, so you finally got tired of her dodging your calls, did you?''

Mac felt the flush crawl up his neck. So he'd been right. She had been avoiding him both here and at the hospital. ''I'd appreciate it if you'd tell her I'm here.''

''I'd be happy to tell her—if she were here. But she's not.''

He might like the woman and could understand her

wanting to protect her friend, but he had no intention of leaving until he saw Rachel. "With all due respect, ma'am, I know Rachel's your friend and I can appreciate your wanting to protect her. But I promise you, I mean no harm. I just want to talk to her."

"And if she were here, I'd tell you. But she isn't."

Growing more frustrated by the minute, Mac set his coffee mug down on the table and stood. "I happen to know she hasn't left for work yet."

"Oh? And how would you know that, Commander?" she asked, a hint of amusement in her voice.

"Because I've been parked outside since oh-four-hundred hours, um, four o'clock this morning, and Rachel hasn't set foot outside this house today."

"You're right, she hasn't set foot outside—today. That's because she isn't here. She's gone to her parents for the weekend."

Still not convinced, Mac asked, "Then what's her car doing out front?"

"I'm using it!" Obviously noting his skeptical expression, she sighed and then began to explain, "Rachel got a flat tire about a week ago and swapped it with the spare in her trunk. Then she forgot about it—until she was ready to leave for her parents' yesterday. She was anxious to get on the road, so I offered to loan her my car since the last thing she needs is to break down on the interstate with P.J. and find herself without a spare. I figured it would be easier for me to get a tire changed in the city than it would be for her to have to deal with a flat between here and Mississippi."

Mac felt as though he'd had the wind kicked out of him. He sank down to the chair Chloe had offered him earlier. "She left town to get away from me, didn't she?"

Chloe's expression softened. "I think she wanted some

time away from everything and everyone so she could think. Rachel was really broken up when you left her two years ago. If it hadn't been for P.J., well I'm not sure she would have come out of it in one piece.''

''I didn't know about the baby,'' Mac told her.

''I know you didn't. I wanted her to tell you, told her I thought she should, but Rachel decided against it. I think she had convinced herself she was over you and that telling you about P.J. would only complicate things for both of you. Then you showed up here out of the blue and, well, I think it shook Rachel.''

''I never meant to,'' Mac informed her. ''It's just that I...I couldn't forget her. And I wanted to see her so badly. That's why I came here that night, and then when I found out about P.J.—''

She patted his hand. ''I know. Not quite what you were expecting,'' she offered. ''I probably should have told you about him when you came here that night looking for Rachel. And who knows, if the little rascal had been awake, I might have. But since he wasn't, I didn't feel it was my place to break the news that you were a daddy. At any rate, now you know.''

''Yeah, now I know.''

She leaned back in her chair, eyed him closely. ''So tell me, Commander, now that you've seen Rachel again and know about P.J., what do you intend to do about it?''

''I want to marry Rachel, be a father to P.J.''

She beamed at him. ''I knew I was right about you.''

Her response left him feeling confused and very much like he'd just given the correct answer on a game show that he'd been unaware he was playing. But rather than say as much, he buried his face in the cup of coffee.

''You know I've always considered one of my strengths to be my ability to see people for who and what they really are.'' She stood and walked over to the kitchen counter to refill her cup, then returned to the table and topped off his own. ''I'm glad I was right about you being a good guy.''

''I, um, thanks,'' he murmured, and took another swig of coffee he really didn't want.

''And I think you're just what Rachel needs. Only she hasn't figured it out yet,'' she informed him as she resumed her seat. She crossed her legs, reached for the sugar and dumped a spoonful into her coffee.

''I'm hoping to change her mind. That's why I came here this morning. I was going to ask her to marry me.''

''I figured as much. But I'm afraid it's going to take more than a few pretty words and a ring to convince her. You've got your work cut out for you. She's wary of you—and rightfully so. You hurt her before.''

''I realize that,'' Mac told her. ''And I know there's P.J. to consider now.''

''True, and I'd shoot you myself if I thought you'd hurt him.''

''It's not my intention to hurt either of them,'' Mac assured her.

Chloe nodded and added still another spoonful of sugar to her cup. ''But convincing Rachel of that isn't your only problem. You have competition.''

Mac narrowed his eyes.

''His name is Alex Jenkins. He's a doctor at the hospital where she works.''

Mac's blood ran cold. He set down the coffee cup before he crushed it in his fist. ''How serious is it?''

''Not as serious as Alex would like it to be,'' she advised him, a distinct bite in her tone.

''You don't like him.''

''What's not to like? He's handsome, rich and a nice

enough guy if you like the blue-blooded, stuffy type. But he's all wrong for Rachel and she's all wrong for him. They don't love each other. There's no spark between them—not the way there was when I saw Rachel with you the other night. If she marries Alex, they'll bore each other to death inside of a month,'' Chloe informed him with more than a little heat in her voice. ''A blind man could see that the two of them don't belong together. But not that idiot Alex. No not *him*. *He* has this image of what he *thinks* a wife should be, and Rachel fits it to a tee. And why wouldn't she?'' Chloe continued as she stirred her coffee viciously. ''She's the perfect lady. Beautiful, sweet, gentle. She's everything Alex thinks he wants.''

It was the crack in her voice on that last statement that had Mac jerking his thoughts from a haze of jealousy and misery. He stared at the woman seated across from him. Her short, dark hair was a tumbled mess, and her brown eyes were brimming with tears. It was the tears that alarmed him. He'd never been able to bide a woman's tears. They made him feel weak, ineffective, a failure. Neither time nor practice had changed that. Just the sight of a female on the verge of tears set off a panic inside him every time. Just like Chloe's near-tears state was doing now. ''Ma'am, are you all right?'' he asked, shoving aside his own frustrations for the moment. ''Chloe,'' he used her name when she failed to answer. He was more fearful of those tears falling than he'd ever been of an enemy during a mission. ''Does this Alex fellow know that you're in love with him?''

''I'm not—'' She swallowed and apparently decided not to bother denying he was right. ''No, he doesn't know,'' she told him. ''And if you so much as breathe a word to the big ox, I really will shoot you.''

"I understand." And he did. For all her bluster, he suspected Chloe Chancellor was a proud woman. "What about Rachel? Does she know how you feel?"

She shook her head. Then took a deep breath. "I've never told her. If she had any idea, she would step aside."

"And that's not what you want?"

"It wouldn't make any difference. As far as Alex is concerned, I'm a flaky artist. I don't fit his wife profile," she replied. "And I can't say that I blame him all that much. I mean, can you imagine me as a doctor's wife?"

He stared at her bright colored robe, the bare feet with silvery nail polish dotted with stars and smiled. "I think you'd make a good doctor's wife. You're kind, funny and bright. And with you around, the good doctor would never be in danger of being bored."

She laughed, and the threat of tears seemed to have passed. "Thanks, Commander. I needed that."

"Happy to be of service, ma'am."

"All right. Enough about my problems. What we need to do is focus on yours—namely, how to convince Rachel to marry you. The way I see it, we need to start by forcing her to spend time with you. To make her see that you're the one that she and P.J. belong with. To do that, we're going to have to use P.J."

Mac sobered. "Ma'am, as much as I want Rachel and P.J. and me to be a family, I'm not going to threaten her with custody of P.J. to get her to marry me."

"Who said anything about threatening her? I'm talking about using the chance to spend time with P.J. to force Rachel to be around you."

Puzzled, Mac said, "That all sounds good, but I don't see how that forces Rachel to spend time in my company, too. All she has to do is let me pick him up or drop him off at my hotel.''

''That's if you were living in a hotel,'' she said, retrieving her cup of coffee. She took a sip, then smiled at him over the rim like the Cheshire Cat. ''What would you say to moving in here?''

Mac blinked. ''Here? You mean you'd let me stay here?''

''Why not? I imagine the hotel where you're staying—even with a government rate—you're paying big bucks this time of year because of the conventions. This is a big house. And there're five bedrooms—two of which are not being used. Renting one of those rooms to you so that you can spend time with your son seems the decent thing to do. Don't you agree?''

''Quite decent,'' Mac told her, and grinned.

''Of course, that will mean you and Rachel are bound to bump into each other on occasion. I mean, it's difficult for people to live in the same house and not see each other. But since you're both adults, I'm sure the two of you can manage. So what do you say, Commander?''

''When do I move in?''

Rachel pulled the Ford Mustang up to the curb in front of the house and shut off the engine. Lord, but it was good to be home, she thought as she unfastened her seat belt and unlocked her car door. She'd needed the break, she admitted. Between the wild schedule at the hospital and Mac's showing up out of the blue, she'd been running on empty both physically and emotionally. She knew it had been cowardly of her to duck Mac's phone calls and then leave town as she had, but she hadn't expected that just seeing him again would resurrect so many feelings inside her. She didn't want to be in love with

Mac McKenna again. She'd had a difficult enough time recovering from her last bout with that particular disease. And she'd been so sure she was over him—until that night on the veranda. For a few moments when he had looked at her, held her in his arms, and kissed her, she'd felt herself weaken. She'd almost believed they might have a chance of making it together.

Until she'd remembered the last time she'd sold herself that fairy tale and the heartache that had followed. Thank heavens she had come to her senses in time. The visit with her parents had been exactly what she'd needed—a much-needed rest and time to put things in perspective where Mac was concerned. But as nice as the time away and the visit with her parents had been, it felt good to be home again.

She opened the rear door of the car and smiled at the sight of her son, who had fallen asleep during the two-hour drive back from the coast. He was so sweet, so beautiful, she thought. To this day, she didn't regret nor would she ever regret the time she'd spent loving Mac. How could she when the result had been a gift this precious? Ducking her head inside the car, she reached out and smoothed back the dark baby curls. "We're home, handsome," she whispered, and proceeded to unfasten the safety belt of his car seat. After slipping his arms through the straps, she lifted the sleeping darling into her arms and began backing out of the car with him.

"Need some help?"

Rachel jerked and banged her skull just inside the top of the car door.

"Rach? Are you okay?" Mac asked, as she made a none-too-graceful exit from the car.

"I'm fine," she snapped even though her head hurt

like blazes. "What are you doing here?" she demanded, taking care not to raise her voice and wake P.J.

"I saw you drive up and thought you might be able to use some help. Looks like this little fellow is down for the count," he remarked as he shut the car door.

"He had a full day and he's a sound sleeper," she replied, still too shocked by the sight of Mac to realize just how inane she must sound.

"Well he looks like he's a load, why don't you let me carry him inside for you?"

And before she could object, Mac had whisked P.J. from her arms and was carrying him up the walkway toward the house. Rachel hurried after him. "I meant what are you doing here?"

"You want to get the door for me? Chloe's not home. She had to run out for a minute. I was working out back."

He was working out back? She unlocked the door and followed Mac inside. "His room is upstairs, the second door to the—"

"I know where it is," he advised her, and walked through the house with a familiarity that made her ill at ease. Rachel hurried inside the room ahead of him and pulled back the comforter on P.J.'s bed.

"He's a real solid little guy," Mac murmured.

Like his father, Rachel thought as she watched Mac place their sleeping son in his bed.

"Should I take off his shoes?"

Rachel nodded and watched as Mac eased off one shoe and then another, with a gentleness that never failed to surprise her, given Mac's large size and choice of profession. She knew from what Mac had told her and from her own research about the fighting unit that meant so much to him, that as a U.S. Navy SEAL Mac was considered an elite warrior, among the best of the best. He'd undergone rigorous training, participated in missions that a normal man couldn't hope to survive. Had Mac lived during the reign of the Roman emperors, she had no doubts that he would have been a champion gladiator.

Yet there he was removing P.J.'s tiny socks with those big, lethal hands with the care of a surgeon. It had been this gentle, caring side of him that snagged her attention the first time she'd seen him. He'd come striding into the hospital emergency room, wearing wet cut-off jeans and a tan George Hamilton would envy. Dismissing the deep gash in his hand, his only concern had been for the two teens who'd been brought in after a waterskiing accident. She had known at once that he was the hero who had jumped into the lake and saved the teenagers from sustaining serious injuries and probably losing their lives. According to the reports, the speedboat's driver had been thrown from the boat, and although the skier had dropped her line, the unmanned boat had been spinning in circles around the hysterical girl. No one had dared go near the boat or the girl for fear of being sliced by the razor-sharp propellor. No one that is except Mac McKenna who had risked his own life to shut off the boat's engines and get the injured teens to safety.

Despite his protests that he was fine, he'd agreed to let the doctor stitch the hand he'd sliced on the boat's engine—but only if Rachel would agree to have coffee with him on her break. Of course, she'd agreed. She'd also agreed to dinner later that evening. And before the weekend was over, she'd been head over heels in love with him.

"Rach?"

Rachel jerked her thoughts back from the past and

stared up at Mac, who was watching her with an expectant expression on his face. "What?"

"I asked if the blanket was enough," he said, keeping his voice to just above a whisper. "Or should I cover him with that bedspread thing, too?"

"No. The blanket is enough. He'll be up soon for dinner, then I'll bathe him and change him into his pajamas."

Mac nodded, then turned and looked down at P.J. Hesitantly he ran his index finger over P.J.'s tiny hand, and the longing in the gesture made her heart swell. Swallowing hard against the sudden emotion, Rachel reminded herself that this time more than just her own feelings were at stake. This time there was P.J. to consider. And while she might be foolish enough to risk her own heart a second time with Mac, she wasn't about to risk her son's. "We need to talk, Mac."

As though sensing her mood, he straightened and stepped away from P.J.'s bed. "Sure, just let me know when you're ready," he said, and without waiting for her to answer, he left the room.

Rachel started to follow when a whimper from P.J.'s bed brought her back to his side. After she settled him and he drifted back to sleep, she turned on the baby monitor, then shut the door quietly behind her to go in search of Mac.

She found him carrying in the last of her things from the car. "You didn't have to do that," she admonished and wanted to wince at the sharpness in her voice. "I mean, I was going to get all that stuff."

"I thought I'd save you the trouble. Where do you want this?" he asked, indicating the portable playpen she had taken to use at her parents.

''There's a storage closet at the top of the stairs. I keep it there. But I can—''

Ignoring her, he took the stairs two at a time with the portable playpen under one arm and her suitcase under the other. Rachel climbed the stairs in his wake. She cut a glance down the hall toward P.J.'s room and frowned when she noted her suitcase now sat outside her own bedroom.

''I wasn't sure what to do with the diaper bag stuff and the shopping bag, so I left them downstairs in the hall. I put the little padded thing with the juice and milk in it inside the fridge.''

''Thank you,'' Rachel said, growing more uneasy by the second at Mac's familiarity with the house.

''No problem.'' He shut the closet door and joined her at the top of the stairs, where he motioned for her to precede him.

She descended the stairs in silence, keenly aware of Mac close behind her. When she reached the landing, she turned and faced him. ''Mac, you want to tell me what's going on?''

''Going on?'' he repeated, all innocence and charm.

She knew the man was far from innocent, and she was determined to resist his charm—no matter how susceptible she might be to it. ''What are you doing here? What is it you think you're going to accomplish by showing up here like this?''

The teasing light in his eyes died as swiftly as the smile on his lips. ''I'm here because you're here and so is my son. I want to be a part of his life and yours. I'm here because I'm hoping I can convince you to give me another chance. I want another chance, Rach,'' he told her, moving closer, mesmerizing her with those blue eyes. ''I want a chance to make things right.''

It was the last statement that broke the seductive spell. "You mean by making an honest woman out of me?" she asked, hanging on to her temper by a thread.

"I wouldn't have put it that way, but yes. I want to marry you, give you and P.J. my name."

Rachel had to grit her teeth to keep from snarling. She held on to her anger, used it to block out some of the pain. "As I said before, I appreciate the offer, but no thanks. In case you haven't noticed, P.J. and I already have a name—mine. We've gotten along just fine with the name Grant and I see no reason to change it."

"Damn it, Rachel, don't twist my words," Mac argued, and followed swiftly behind her as she started across the hall toward the front door.

"Listen, I've had a long day and I'd like to unpack before P.J. wakes up and I have to get him dinner. So if you don't mind, I'd like you to go."

"But, you don't understand. I—"

"I understand that you're leaving—now." She yanked open the door and found a startled Chloe standing on the other side with her arms loaded with shopping bags and an elbow poised to hit the doorbell.

"Rachel, honey, you're back. Commander, sugar, give me a hand."

"I'll get it," Rachel said grabbing at some of the packages. "Mac's leaving."

Chloe blinked. "Leaving? But where's he going?"

"Back to his hotel, his SEAL team, to Timbuktu for all I care. But he's going."

"But, Rachel—" Chloe began.

"I know you mean well, but stay out of this, Chlo. Goodbye, Mac," she said and would have given him a shove out the door if she'd thought she had any prayer of moving a man as solid as a mountain.

''Didn't you tell her?'' Chloe asked.

''I didn't get a chance.''

''Tell me what?'' Rachel asked, that uneasy feeling she'd had earlier coming back full force as her gaze volleyed from Chloe to Mac and back again.

''That I moved in here two days ago. I'm staying in the spare bedroom down the hall from you.''

Four

"**R**achel, honey, be reasonable," Chloe pleaded.

Rachel whirled around. "I am being reasonable. I don't want him here, and you should never have let him move in here without talking to me about it first."

"She's right, ma'am. Why don't I just go—"

"Commander, sugar, butt out."

"Yes, butt out," Rachel echoed her friend's sentiments. "This is between me and Chloe."

Mac started to argue that *he* was the issue between them, but with both women shooting him murderous looks, he opted for silence instead. He'd never seen Rachel so steamed before. In the time they'd been together, he'd rarely heard her so much as raise her voice and then only if she were frustrated. Even the other night when he knew she was angry with him for showing up as he did and making that halfhearted offer to do right by her, she'd been truly miffed. But her cheeks hadn't been hot with temper, her gray eyes hadn't been flashing with fire. Not the way they were now. Now that he thought about it, Chloe's description of Rachel as sweet tempered and a lady had been right on the mark as far as he was concerned. But there wasn't anything sweet tempered or ladylike in the way Rachel was standing toe-to-toe with her friend yelling at her.

"Don't you dare use my being away as an excuse. That thing sitting over there is a telephone and I know that you know how to use it. You should have called me."

"And do what? Have you tell me not to let him move in?" Chloe returned with a very unladylike snort. "Honey, why do you think I didn't call?"

Rachel made some sound—something between a scream and an oath—and stamped her foot. "You're impossible!"

"Why, thank you, sweetie," Chloe replied calmly.

"It wasn't a compliment, Chloe."

Mac watched, somewhat fascinated, as Chloe let that one roll right off her and pressed ahead. "Now if you'll just settle down, honey, I'm sure you'll see that my letting the commander move in here was the perfect solution to your problem."

"His moving in here *is* the problem," Rachel told her, her voice rising another notch. "And the way I see to fix that problem is for *him,*" she said, whipping an accusatory finger in his direction, "to march upstairs, pack his things and hightail it out of here."

"She's right, ma'am," he said. "I appreciate your trying to help, but maybe my moving in here wasn't such a good idea after all. Given how Rachel feels, I think it's best if I leave. I'll go get my gear." He paused, slid a glance toward Rachel. "If it's all right, I'll give you a call and see about setting up something so that I can see P.J." Then he turned and headed toward the door, intent on clearing out before any more harsh words were shed.

"You stop right there, Commander," Chloe ordered.

Mac hesitated at the steel edge in her voice. "Ma'am?"

"After all the trouble I've gone to to help you, you are not going to bail on me now. Not until this is settled."

"It is settled," Rachel informed her. "He's leaving."

"He is not," Chloe countered.

"Ladies—"

"Quiet," both women snapped.

"This is still my house, and I invited him to stay here as my guest," Chloe informed Rachel.

"You're right. It is your house," Rachel told her, this time her voice softer, her chin tipped up slightly higher. "You've been so generous to me and P.J., allowing us to live here that sometimes I forget that it really isn't our home. And of course, you're free to have anyone you want stay here as your guest." She turned toward him and in that same soft, regal way, she said, "There's no need for you to leave, Mac. P.J. and I will go."

"Rach, no," Mac began. "You don't have to do that. I'm going."

Chloe swore. "Oh, for pity's sake, don't you dare pull that on me, Rachel Grant. This is as much your home as it is mine, and you know it. Why I...I..."

Her voice broke and Mac felt sweat gather between his shoulder blades at the sight of tears filling her eyes. He was gauging how quickly he could get packed and out the door when the two women started to hug and talk at once.

"Don't you know I'd be lost without you and P.J.

here?'' Chloe said. ''I love you, you idiot. And that little monster of yours, too. You guys are my family.''

''I'm sorry, Chlo,'' Rachel told her with a sniffle.

It was the sniffle that had Mac edging toward the door, eager to make his escape. And the very first thing he was going to do once he got back to the hotel—that is if he could get them to take him back—was to call his mother and thank her for giving him only brothers to deal with.

''Oh, no you don't, Commander,'' Chloe called out just as he made it to the doorway. ''You're not sneaking out of here after all the trouble you've caused. You get those cute buns of yours back over here now.''

''With all due respect, ma'am, I think I should leave.''

''You do, and I'll take it as a personal insult and consider it a rebuff to my hospitality.''

''Oh, for pity's sake, Chloe, leave the man alone. You heard him. He *wants* to go.''

''Is that right, Commander, sugar? You want to leave?''

''I think it would be best if I did,'' Mac offered.

''Best for whom?'' Chloe countered.

''For everyone,'' Mac replied.

''Including your son?'' she asked.

''I'm doing it for my son,'' Mac informed her.

''Really? So earlier when you told me how you wanted to be a real father to him, how you wanted to spend some time with him, get to know him and try to make up for missing those first eighteen months of his life. All of that was just talk? You didn't mean any of it?''

''I meant every word of it,'' Mac ground out in reply, not at all pleased to have his words or his feelings about his son questioned. ''But what I don't want is to cause any upheaval in his life. Obviously, given Rachel's feelings, my staying here will do that. I still intend to see

P.J. I just won't be able to spend as much time with him as I'd hoped.''

''I guess you're right,'' Chloe offered in an about-face that Mac didn't trust at all. She walked behind an over-stuffed chair, trailed her fingers across the back. ''I suppose after the first few times you pick him up for a visit, he probably won't cry when you bring him to some dingy hotel room so that he can stay with you.''

Mac frowned. ''I don't want to make him cry. I-I'll just visit with him here. Maybe in your backyard. If that's okay.''

''But you can't do that,'' Chloe said innocently. ''You said yourself your being here makes Rachel uncomfortable. No, no. I'm sure P.J. will get used to it. And if he takes his favorite blanket and teddy with him, he probably won't cry too much when you put him down for his nap.''

''I could bring him back here for his nap, and then pick him up again later.'' The last thing he wanted to do was to make P.J. unhappy.

Chloe shook her head. ''That wouldn't work, either. He'd probably just get even more confused. No. You and Rachel are right. You might as well let him get used to zipping back and forth between the two of you while he's young.''

''Oh, put a sock in it, Chloe. You've made your point,'' Rachel told her, then shifted her gaze to him. ''If you want to stay here until you go back to your team, then you can stay.''

''Thanks.''

''And, you,'' she said to Chloe, pointing that accusatory finger at her. ''I know what you're up to, and I'm telling you this little scheme of yours isn't going to work.''

"Why, Rachel, honey, whatever are you talking about?" Chloe asked.

"I'm talking about your attempt to play matchmaker. And don't bother denying it," she continued when Chloe started to object. "You think that just because Mac and I were…were involved at one time that if we're living under the same roof for a couple of weeks that something's going to happen again. Well, you're wrong, my meddling friend. Nothing is going to happen between us. Now if you'll both excuse me, I need to check on my son."

Still a bit shell-shocked by this new, temperamental Rachel, Mac continued to stare at the door through which she'd exited for several seconds—only to find himself suddenly being hugged by a squealing Chloe.

"I knew it! I knew it! Oh, Commander, sugar, I was right. She's still crazy about you."

Puzzled, Mac held the colorful woman smiling up at him at arm's length. "Uh, ma'am, I hate to burst your bubble. But I'd say crazy to be rid of me is more like it. And to be honest, I can't say that I blame her. Maybe I really should move back to the hotel."

"I don't believe this. Are you wimping out on me, Commander? Where's your fighting spirit? I thought you polar bears were supposed to be real tough guys?"

"I don't want to fight with Rachel," Mac informed her. "I've hurt her enough already. And it's SEAL, ma'am. Navy SEALs," he corrected, but he suspected she already knew that.

"SEALs, bears, whatever," she said dismissing his comments with a wave of her hand. "It's not a question of your fighting *with* Rachel, Commander. It's whether you're willing to fight *for* her. So what's it going to be? You going to stay and fight for her and your son? Or are you going to throw in the towel and let her marry a man she doesn't love because she thinks P.J. needs a father?''

Everything inside Mac went cold at the thought of Rachel with someone else, of his son calling another man Daddy. If Rachel was going to marry anyone and if P.J. was going to call any man Daddy, he damn well intended for it to be him. With the decision made, Mac grinned. ''You're a piece of work, Chloe Chancellor. Thanks.'' And for once he had the pleasure of catching her off guard when he swooped her up and planted a noisy kiss on her mouth. Then leaving her looking more than a little flustered and unsteady on her feet, he turned and whistled as he headed upstairs.

''Chloe, I'm home,'' Rachel called out as she entered the house a few afternoons later. After hanging up her jacket and setting down her handbag, she scooped up the mail resting on the table in the foyer and started toward the den. ''Chloe, did you hear me? I'm home.''

When she was met with only silence, she glanced up from the mail she had been perusing and noted that the den was empty. Somewhat surprised since Chloe had agreed to pick P.J. up from the sitter for her, Rachel headed toward the kitchen, sure she'd find her friend and son there. She didn't find them. But what she did find was the smell of something wonderful cooking.

''Oh, bless you, Chloe,'' she murmured when she lifted the lid and found a thick Italian sauce with meatballs simmering. She inhaled deeply, and the spicy scents of oregano and thyme made her mouth water. The grumble from her belly quickly reminded her that she had worked straight through lunch at the hospital that day. The toast and coffee she'd chosen for breakfast in order to escape starting another day off sharing the kitchen with

Mac hadn't been nearly enough to sustain her hunger pangs.

At least this was one meal she wouldn't have to share with Mac, Rachel thought, relieved to have learned from Chloe that Mac had said he'd be out all day. With any luck, she, Chloe and P.J. could have an early dinner and then she'd disappear to her room before Mac came home.

Rachel frowned, disliking the fact that it seemed cowardly for her to avoid Mac as she was doing. Just as quickly she reminded herself that self-preservation had to be her primary focus. Because despite what she'd told Chloe, she was very much afraid that her friend's scheme to throw them together was working. It worried her. More than that, it scared her. If she'd had any doubts that she was still susceptible to him, they'd been put to rest during the past few days. Every time she saw him with P.J., watched her son bask in his father's attention and watched Mac fall under their child's spell, it became more and more difficult for her not to think, not to wonder how it would be if they could be a real family. Added to that already-heart-twisting mix was Mac's desire for her. He made no attempt to disguise the fact that he wanted her. If anything, the electrical charge between them was even stronger now than it had been two years ago. But it was more than desire this time, there was a yearning she sensed whenever she caught him watching her. The combination and his obvious affection for P.J. was making it more difficult for her not to give him that second chance he had asked for. Yet how could she, knowing that he would be with her out of a sense of honor and duty to P.J. and not because he loved her? The simple fact was, she couldn't. Not and still be able to look at herself in the mirror each morning.

No, she told herself. It was far better to avoid leading

with her heart as she had the last time she and Mac Mc-
Kenna tangled. Instead she would give him the time he
wanted with P.J. and trust him to keep his word to remain
a part of their son's life. As for her, she'd simply do her
best to avoid spending any more time with him than nec-
essary.

Suddenly realizing that she'd been standing in front of
the stove wasting time thinking about Mac when she
should have been looking for P.J. and Chloe, Rachel covered the pot of meatballs and started to head upstairs
when a blur of red wool outside the breakfast window
caught her eye. Moving into the cozy little breakfast
nook, she stared outside into the big backyard and saw
them. Mac and P.J. in the midst of a huge pile of oak
and maple leaves. Or rather Mac was seated in the center
of the pile of leaves while P.J., with his cheeks pink with
laughter and his little fists filled with leaves, was dropping those leaves on his father.

Rachel's throat went tight. She pressed her fingers
against the cool windowpane as she watched her son
squeal with delight when Mac snatched him up and
dumped leaves atop his head. Then the two of them were
laughing as they rolled around in the leaves together. Rachel's eyes began to sting at the simple beauty of the
moment, and she realized that by keeping the news about
P.J. from Mac, she had stolen other moments like these
from her son. She loved P.J. He was her world. Yet Mac
had been right. While she could give P.J. many things,
fulfill his physical needs and most of his emotional ones,
she couldn't give him moments like these—moments between a father and son.

At the sound of a tap against the house, Rachel opened
her eyes and stared out the window at Mac. He was still
sprawled on the ground with leaves scattered in his hair

and more leaves clinging to his navy-blue sweater and jeans. His lips were curved into that impossible-to-resist grin, and his eyes were twinkling with laughter. Another popping sound against the house had Rachel jerk her gaze downward where her darling son was standing under the window attempting to fire acorns at her. She stared at the miniature version of Mac and began to laugh. After two more misfires, Rachel opened the window. "Hey, handsome, what are you up to?" she asked her son.

"Help Daddy wake weaves," he said.

Rachel arched her brow, looked over at Mac. "Is that so? Looks to me like you and Daddy made a big mess."

Mac held up his hands in an innocent gesture. "Hey don't look at me. Talk to pistol-packing Pete there. He started off by picking up acorns and putting them in his bucket. Then he decided it would be more fun to dump them on me. When he ran out of acorns, he started with the leaves."

"And I wonder where he got the idea from?" she teased.

"I think maybe I'd better take the Fifth on that."

"I think maybe you'd better," Rachel told him, and then she laughed again. She couldn't help it. It felt good to laugh, she admitted. She hadn't realized until that moment that she'd laughed far too little under the strain of the past week. From the sudden darkening in Mac's eyes, she suspected that he realized it, too.

"Mommy, come play," P.J. told her.

Rachel pulled her gaze away from Mac and stared down at her son. "Oh, sweetie, I don't think so. I'm still in my uniform. You and Daddy play."

"Mommy come play," P.J. insisted.

"Come on, Rach. It's actually pretty nice out here— not too cold. We've probably got another hour of sunlight. Why don't you go put on some jeans, and P.J. and I will teach you how we men rake leaves.''

Rachel tilted her head. ''As opposed to how we women rake leaves? I didn't realize there was a difference.''

Mac made a snorting sound. P.J. did a sweet imitation of the sound that resulted in baby spittle on Mac. Ignoring the faux pas, Mac went on, ''Of course there's a difference. Women make those little sissy piles of leaves that you spend half the day walking around the yard bagging up. While we tough macho men, we make one big pile and save half the time. Right, pardner?'' he asked P.J. as he slipped the little boy from his shoulders.

''Wight, parner.''

''And then when we finish raking, we do this.''

Tucking P.J. under his arm like a football, Mac dove into the leaves, landing on his back and cushioning P.J.'s fall as he pulled him down on top of his chest. P.J. squealed, his baby laughter echoing on the autumn air.

''Do again, Daddy. Do again,'' P.J. urged. Anchoring his fists in Mac's hair, he began bouncing on Mac's chest.

''Have a heart, Rach. Come out here and help me before this boy of ours leaves me bald.''

Rachel hesitated, torn by the desire to join them and the voice in the back of her head that warned she was getting in too deep.

Mac tumbled himself and P.J. in the bed of leaves. And amidst their laughter, his eyes once more sought hers. ''Come on, Rach. Come join us.''

Rachel ignored the voice in her head that reminded her of the last time she'd fallen under Mac McKenna's spell—only to discover that while he desired her, he didn't love her. Instead she followed her heart, and after swiftly changing into a pair of old jeans and sweatshirt, she raced down the stairs and out into the backyard.

Mac was busily raking the leaves back into the giant pile while P.J., with a bright green-and-yellow plastic rake that was almost as big as he was, managed to rake, then scatter, the same fistful of leaves over and over.

"Got another rake?" she asked as she walked toward them.

P.J. turned around, looked up at her and grinned. Surprisingly Mac didn't acknowledge her. Not sure what to make of it, she moved to within a few yards of him. Mac whipped around, and from the expression on his face, he seemed surprised to see her. Telling herself she was imagining things, Rachel offered a smile and asked, "If you've got another rake, I'll give you a hand."

"The truth is, I think we've about got it. But you can help me bag it up."

"All right," she said, a little disappointed. "There should be some bags in the gardening shed."

She turned and started toward the far corner of the yard for the bags, only to shriek when she found herself being scooped up into Mac's arms. He carried her back to where the leaves had once again been piled into a big bed.

"What do you say, pardner?" he addressed P.J. while holding her aloft. "Think it's time for your mommy to take a fall."

"Don't you dare, McKenna," she warned him, but ruined it by bursting into laughter.

"Mommy fall. Mommy fall," P.J. cried out.

"Mac! Mac, I'm warning you," she told him as he began swinging her.

"Sorry, Rach. You heard my pardner there. You'd better let go of my neck, or we'll go down together and I'll probably end up on top of you. Not that I'd mind being on top of you,'' he whispered in her ear. And the nearness of his mouth, the feel of being in his arms sent heat pooling in her belly, down between her thighs.

He made a growling noise somewhere deep in his throat. ''You keep looking at me like that, and there won't be any option. I want you, Rachel. So much that I can hardly breathe.''

''Mommy fall, Daddy. Mommy fall,'' P.J. called from somewhere below, and Rachel jerked herself back from the brink.

''You just wait, buster,'' she told her son as she attempted to shake off the seductive spell she'd been under. ''Mommy's going to get you,'' she warned, and reached out, making wiggly fingers at him.

Mac chose that moment to toss her into the pile of leaves. Then he picked up a squealing P.J. and tossed him after her. Rachel surfaced, spitting leaves from her mouth and gathering P.J. close. He giggled as the two of them made plans for Mac. He played along with the game, pretended to be surprised when they each dragged him over and pushed him into the pile of leaves.

By the time the sun began to set forty-five minutes later, Rachel's jaw ached from laughing and she suspected she'd be finding bruises on various parts of her body for the next few days.

''I think that's it,'' Mac told her. ''I'll haul these bags into the gardener's shed for now. If you and Chloe decide you want to use them in the flower beds for mulch, just let me know. I can lay it down for you while I'm here.''

''Sounds good,'' Rachel told him and swiped a strand of hair that had fallen from her braid away from her cheek.

''Hang on a second,'' Mac told her. He moved closer

and, taking a handkerchief from the back pocket of his jeans, he wiped at a spot on her cheek. He was so close, Rachel could see the shadow of new whiskers on his chin, the fullness of his mouth, the sinfully long, dark lashes, the blue rim that circled the iris of his eyes. And she could smell him—the scent of the leaves, the grass and sweat that clung to his skin, and that distinct spicy scent that belonged only to Mac.

The hand working on her cheek stilled while the hand holding her chin tightened. His nostrils flared. Rachel lifted her gaze, looked into his eyes. His gaze slid to her mouth, and she sucked in a breath, waited.

"Rach," he said her name like a prayer, and began to lower his head.

She closed her eyes, already anticipating the heat of his mouth, the taste of him, when P.J. screamed.

Five

"**I** can't believe I was so careless," Mac said, furious with himself that P.J. had fallen and cut his finger on the rake that he'd left lying on the ground.

"Mac, it was an accident. Accidents happen. Besides, he's a tough guy, aren't you, sweetie?"

"I tuf guy," P.J. echoed from his perch atop the kitchen counter as he watched his mother tend to his wound. Now that the cut had been cleaned and the damage assessed, the tears had stopped. Yet one look at the tear streaks on the little boy's cheeks had Mac's chest tightening again.

"There you go," Rachel told P.J. as she finished applying a Barney Band-Aid to his finger and gave it a kiss. "Good as new."

Obviously, the purple dinosaur was a favorite, Mac surmised, given the smile spreading on P.J.'s face as he held up his finger and admired it.

"I really am sorry, Rach," Mac told her again.

"Mac, it's all right, really. This isn't the first time this guy has had an accident, and I'm sure it won't be the last. And as accidents go, this one was pretty minor."

"Yeah, well it didn't feel minor to me. My blood ran cold when I heard him scream."

"Believe me, I understand," she told him. "I've had a few years shaved off my life on more than one occasion since he started walking. You should have seen me when he fell and busted his mouth on the coffee table."

"Ouch," Mac said wincing at the thought of P.J. being hurt.

"Ouch is right. You'd have thought Chloe was the trained nurse the way she took charge. I, on the other hand, was a total ninny. I mean, I nearly lost it when I saw blood coming from that sweet little mouth."

"Can't say that I'd blame you. I'm sure I would have lost it."

Rachel smiled at him, and the way she looked at him set off a strange longing in him for more moments like this one. As though she sensed it, too, and was confused by it, she looked away. "Yes, well, I imagine we'll both need to toughen up, because this little guy seems to have a way of finding ways to get in trouble. Don't you, sweetie?"

P.J. grinned at her. "Barney," he told her, and held up his finger.

"That's right. Barney," she said, and kissed the finger again.

"Daddy kiss," he said, and held the finger out to Mac.

Hearing P.J. call him Daddy sent emotion whirling through Mac. Not sure how to deal with these feelings, he remained silent as he pressed a kiss to the bandaged little finger.

"All better?" Rachel asked.

"Better," P.J. told her, and when Rachel started to reach for him, he said, "No, Daddy hold."

Mac's insides turned to jelly in that moment. He reached for his son, held him close, and when the little boy put his arms around his neck and hugged him, Mac knew he was a goner. In that moment he wondered how he could ever have thought he would want to go through life without a child. His throat was so thick with emotion he didn't dare speak for fear his voice would break.

Rachel must have sensed some of what he was feeling, because she eyed him warily. "It's getting late. I need to see about fixing his dinner."

"Sure," Mac said, and handed P.J. over to Rachel. "Chloe said P.J. likes spaghetti, so I cooked up some meatballs for dinner."

"*You* cooked dinner?"

"Yeah. You have a problem with that?"

"No. Not at all. It's just that I assumed Chloe had cooked," Rachel replied.

Mac went to the stove, checked on the pot of simmering red gravy. "She had some kind of meeting to attend about a fund-raiser next month. So I told her I'd cook."

"I see."

He replaced the lid on the pot, turned off the burner, then went about checking to see that the spaghetti he'd cooked remained warm. "Looks like P.J. inherited your penchant for Italian food."

"Probably because I craved it a lot while I was pregnant," Rachel told him. "I didn't realize you knew how to cook."

"Probably because we spent very little time in the kitchen," he said, and caught the flush of color to Rachel's cheeks. "But the truth is, my culinary skills are limited. Spaghetti and meatballs happen to be among the few things that I can cook.''

"It smells good,'' she said, but he noted that she avoided looking at him.

"It tastes even better,'' he told her. "Everything's ready. I've got a salad in the fridge. All I have to do is heat the bread.''

"Did Chloe say how long she would be?''

"No. But I'm sure she won't mind if we go ahead and eat without her.'' When Rachel hesitated, Mac said, "It's only dinner, Rach. And you yourself said, P.J.'s got to eat.''

"Eat,'' P.J. parroted, forgetting all about his Barney Band-Aid and making a beeline for his chair.

Mac chuckled. "Sounds to me like it's settled.''

Rachel's lips twitched and some of the wariness left her eyes. "Sounds like it. I'll set the table.''

Forty minutes later Mac sat back in his chair, cradling his wineglass in his hands, and watched Rachel who was doing her best to clean P.J.'s hands and face. When she grabbed for yet another napkin, Mac chuckled.

"I'm glad one of us finds this amusing,'' she told him.

"Sorry,'' he replied, even though he didn't really mean it. "It looks to me like he's wearing most of his dinner. Are you sure any of that spaghetti even made it into his mouth?''

The comment made Rachel laugh, and some of the stress that had been in her eyes when they'd sat down to the meal seemed to have disappeared. "I certainly hope so. Otherwise, we're both going to hear about it soon enough. Our son has never been shy about letting me know when he's hungry.''

Our son.

Mac replayed the words in his head, felt that swell of emotion and pride again. And he realized that, for the first time since waking up in the hospital after the explosion and finding out his hearing was damaged, he had gone more than a few hours without worrying about what he would do with his life if he were forced to resign his commission.

"P.J., no!"

Mac yanked his attention back to Rachel and burst into laughter at the sight of P.J. slapping both hands into what was left of his spaghetti and splattering tomato sauce on himself, Rachel and the table.

Rachel glared at him.

"Sorry," Mac offered. But seeing Rachel with a dollop of tomato sauce on her nose and a strand of spaghetti clinging to her cheek made him ruin the apology by bursting into laughter again.

Obviously aware that he had done something entertaining, P.J. splatted his hands into the plate again, causing his mother to shriek. Unable to help himself, Mac laughed even harder.

"Let's see if you think this is funny, too," Rachel told him and before he had a chance to reply, she fired a chunk of garlic bread at him.

The bread hit him square in the forehead, then plopped into the plate of spaghetti in front of him with a distinct splat that sprayed the red tomato sauce across the front of his U.S. Navy sweatshirt.

"Oh, my God! I can't believe I just did that," Rachel said and clapped a hand over her mouth as though horrified by her actions.

"Neither can I," Mac said, and flicked a finger of sauce from the front of his sweatshirt and cleaned it with his tongue. "I guess it's my turn now." Grinning at Rachel, he reached for a slice of the garlic bread.

"Now, Mac. You don't want to set a bad example for P.J., do you?" Rachel asked as she scooted back her chair and started to scramble out of range.

Mac caught her on the shoulder as she started to flee. Obviously thinking this was a new game, P.J. squealed when his mother made a grab at the bread missile that hit her and prepared to fire it right back at him.

No fool, Mac ducked at the same time, the kitchen door opened.

"What on earth is going on—"

The guy standing in the doorway fell silent as the bread hit him in the chest.

"Alex!"

Suddenly the laughter died on Mac's lips as he stared at the tall fair-haired man standing in the doorway and looking at Rachel as though she'd just grown a second head.

"Rachel! What on earth is going on here?" Alex demanded. "What's happened to your clothes? And what is that you've got all over your face?"

Looking shell-shocked, Rachel turned beet red. She swiped her cheek with the sleeve of her sweatshirt and managed to smear the tomato sauce even more. "I'm sorry. I...we..."

"Oh, for pity's sake, Alex. Lighten up," Chloe ordered as she sauntered into the room, a wicked gleam in her eye as she surveyed the mess. "From the looks of this place, we obviously missed a great time."

"You *would* think something so childish is fun," Alex chided.

Chloe circled back to face the doctor and got right in his face. "You know, that's always been your problem,

Alex. You're so busy living up to that respectable Jenkins name, you never did learn the first thing about having fun.''

"As opposed to you, who has made the pursuit of fun your primary purpose in life," Alex fired back.

"If that's your way of saying I know how to have a good time, you're right," Chloe countered.

"Oh, I'd say you'd qualify as an expert," Alex told Chloe. "In fact, I suspect you could give a course at Tulane on the subject."

"Why thank you, Alex, honey," she said, and gave his cheek a pat. "If you should ever decide you want a few lessons," she continued, her voice dropping huskily. "Let me know. I'll be happy to teach you."

Caught up in the byplay between the pair—and particularly the way Alex got all flustered when Chloe got too close—Mac failed to notice for several moments that Chloe had redirected her focus on him. "Commander, sugar," she said. "You do know that you're wearing spaghetti, don't you?"

"Yes, ma'am."

"Rachel, are you going to explain what's going on here?" Alex repeated.

Something dark and primitive clutched inside Mac at the man's proprietary tone with Rachel. Mac took a step toward him. "We just finished dinner," Mac told him. "And as Chloe has already observed, we were in the midst of a little food fight."

"And just who are you?" Alex asked him.

"Mac. Mac McKenna."

"*You're* Chloe's house guest?"

"That's right," Mac said. "Is that a problem?"

Alex slanted a reproving look Chloe's way, and for the first time ever, the outrageous redhead actually flushed.

"No. It's just that when Chloe mentioned she had an old friend of the family visiting, I was left with the distinct impression that you were a great deal older."

"Sorry to disappoint you…Alec, wasn't it?"

"Alex," the other man corrected. "Dr. Alex Jenkins. I'm a close friend of Rachel's. And Chloe's, too, of course."

Mac shook the man's hand and noted, for a man who spent his days in a doctor's office and hospital, Alex Jenkins had a strong grip. "Then I guess that's something we have in common because I'm also a friend of Rachel's, as well as Chloe's."

Apparently not happy at being ignored, P.J. started to fuss. "Out! Out," he said and held up his arms.

"All right, sweetie," Rachel replied and started to reach for him.

"No, Mommy. Daddy. Want Daddy," P.J. insisted.

"P.J.," Rachel began to object.

"It's all right, Rachel. We've been through this before. The boy doesn't know any better, and I really don't mind. If you could wipe his hands and face, I'll be happy to take him."

"Sorry to disappoint you," Mac said through clenched teeth. "But I don't think P.J. was referring to you."

As though to prove his point, P.J. held out his arms to Mac and said, "Daddy, out!"

The special bond and affection he had already begun to feel for the little guy exploded into full-fledged love in that instant. "Daddy's right here, pardner," Mac said and scooped P.J. up into his arms, hugging his tomato-and spaghetti-soiled body close.

Alex narrowed his gaze and volleyed it from Mac to P.J. and back again.

"Strong resemblance, isn't there?" Mac asked, feeling

ten feet tall as he held his son and stared at the man who, according to Chloe, had designs on marrying Rachel. "I'm sorry, Alex, did I forget to mention that I also happen to be P.J.'s father?"

The entire scenario had been straight out of her worst nightmare. Her former lover boldly announcing to the man she'd been dating that he was not only her child's father, but that he was living under the same roof with her. "I'm sorry, Alex. About your pants, about everything."

"Forget about the pants, Rachel. Why didn't you tell me about McKenna? Didn't you think I would want to know?"

What could she say? The truth—that since Mac had showed up on her doorstep she had barely given Alex a thought? "I meant to tell you. I honestly did, it's just that...everything's been so confused since Mac arrived, I just never got around to it. I'm sorry you had to find out this way."

"Yes, well, I guess I should have realized something was bothering you. I've barely seen you lately. It's the reason I accepted Chloe's invitation to come by for coffee after our meeting tonight."

"Thanks for understanding," she told him, her thoughts no longer on Alex but on her son and the man upstairs with him. When she realized she hadn't heard a word Alex had said to her, Rachel gave up pretending. "Forgive me, Alex. But I really do need to go check on P.J. Please stay and have that coffee Chloe promised you. Chloe, would you mind?"

"Not at all," her friend assured her.

"But Rachel—"

"Go on, honey. Take care of P.J.," Chloe told her as she linked her arm with Alex's. "I'll take care of Alex."

"Thanks, Chlo."

"Did I happen to mention that I baked a Dutch apple pie this afternoon?" Chloe asked. "Why don't I serve you up a slice to go with that coffee while I see what I can do about the stain on your pants?"

Evidently Chloe's pie did the trick, Rachel thought as she dashed out the door, because the last thing she heard was Alex's refusal to strip off the pants. Shaking her head at her friend's antics, Rachel dismissed them from her thoughts as she headed for the stairs.

Determined to give Mac a piece of her mind for humiliating her as he had, Rachel marched up the stairs. If she lived to be a hundred, she would never forget the look of shock on Alex's face at Mac's announcement that he was P.J.'s father. And if that hadn't been bad enough, P.J. had wrapped his little arms around Alex's pants leg to say good-night and left behind ugly blotches of tomato sauce and spaghetti on the expensive designer slacks.

And it was all Mac's fault. He was the one who had put her son up to it. After putting P.J. down so he could kiss her and his Aunt Chloe good-night, it had been Mac who had suggested that P.J. give Alex a good-night hug, too. Rachel groaned as she relived that moment over again. To his credit, Alex had assured her it was no big deal, but all she could see were the ugly dark stains left on those lovely gray trousers. Not that it had bothered Mac in the least, she fumed. No, he'd offered a half-hearted, "Oh what a shame, such nice pants," and then had scooped up P.J. and headed upstairs with him.

Well, he wasn't going to get away with it, Rachel promised herself as she cleared the landing at the top of the stairs. Following the sound of P.J.'s laughter, she headed down the hall toward the bathroom, where she found the door ajar.

Mac was kneeling in front of the tub with his back to her, sans his sweatshirt. "Okay, big guy, let me see those toes."

The picture he made bathing P.J., combined with her baby's delighted laughter, nearly undid her. Rachel shook it off, reminded herself just how much this man had embarrassed her just a short time ago. She stepped into the room. Remembering how sharp Mac's sense of hearing was, she braced herself for him to make some remark, acknowledging her presence. It had been one of the things that unnerved her when they'd been together in the past—his ability to hear and sense the slightest of sounds. It was as though he were somehow in tune with the elements and could hear the air itself stir. After a moment when he had failed to comment on her presence, Rachel frowned. Either Mac was slipping or the racket P.J. was making in the tub with his toys had managed to drown out her approach. No matter, she thought, determined to say her piece. "Well, I certainly hope you're proud of yourself, Mac McKenna."

Mac's shoulders stiffened for a fraction of a second, then he resumed swooping his hand through the water like a boat toward P.J. "As a matter of fact, I am."

"What?" Rachel countered, taken aback by his reply. "Don't you at least have the decency to feel a little guilty for what you did?"

"What's to feel guilty about? I managed to get this little guy of ours clean, didn't I? I mean, he even had spaghetti in his ears and diaper."

Rachel made a strangled sound in her throat. "I'm not talking about P.J., and you know it. I'm talking about your behavior downstairs."

''Now you just hang on a second, darling. You're the one who volunteered to clean the kitchen since I cooked, remember? So don't go blaming me for skipping out on the dishes. Besides, I thought your pal Alex would lend you a hand. Don't tell me he's gone already.''

''No, he is not gone. He is downstairs with Chloe.''

''Then you'll have lots of help.''

Before she could catch herself, Rachel stomped her foot. ''You know very well I'm not talking about the dishes, Mac. I'm talking about your behavior toward Alex. It was bad enough the way you announced that you were P.J.'s father. But to use P.J. the way you did—''

He jerked his head in her direction, shot her a furious glance. ''I didn't and wouldn't use my son,'' he informed her.

''All right. Maybe you didn't use him, but you encouraged him to hug Alex, knowing that he was dirty. And you ruined Alex's pants. It was a...a childish thing to do, Mac.''

''Okay, pardner, lean your head back so we can get the rest of that soap out of your hair,'' he told P.J. Using the spray nozzle, he began rinsing P.J.'s hair with that same gentleness that always astonished Rachel, given his size and occupation. ''For your information, Ms. Grant, I was trying to be thoughtful. I didn't want the guy to feel slighted when P.J. gave everyone else a good-night kiss but Alex. I could have easily done without having my son wasting his hugs on the guy, and I sure as hell wasn't happy to hear that P.J. had called him Daddy in the past.''

Rachel paused, not sure what to make of his answer. He made it all sound so reasonable, yet she had sensed Mac's instant dislike of Alex. Feeling confused, Rachel remained silent a moment, and tried to sort out her feelings.

"Anyway, how was I to know that the guy was wearing an Armani suit?"

Rachel bit her lip. She couldn't exactly fault him on that one as she hadn't known it was an Armani suit, either—not until Chloe pointed it out. Not that it mattered. What mattered was that she had been fairly sure Mac had insisted P.J. hug Alex in a deliberate attempt to embarrass the other man. But what if she was wrong? Was she being unfair to Mac?

"Okay, pal. Let's get you out before you shrivel up like a prune." He hit the drain on the tub and as the water gurgled down the drain, he wrapped P.J. in a fluffy blue towel and lifted him out of the tub. His back still to her, he placed P.J. on the rug he'd been kneeling on and proceeded to dry him. "You want to hand me a diaper?"

Once she'd done so, Mac set about dressing P.J. for bed. It was a ritual that until recently she had handled alone—except on those occasions when she had to pull a night shift at the hospital and Chloe filled in for her.

"I still don't know why you're so steamed at me, but hey, if you think it's my fault that the guy's pants got a little dirty, I'll have him send me the cleaning bill."

"That's not the point, Mac," Rachel argued.

"All right, then, why don't you tell me what the point *is?*"

"The point is that you—"

Mac pulled P.J. up on his feet, then stood himself and turned to face her.

Rachel's mouth went dry. Her brain turned to mush. The sight of Mac standing there bare from the waist up with his jeans slung low on his hips sent all thoughts straight out of her head save one. Mac was gorgeous. He was even more gorgeous than she'd remembered—with those linebacker shoulders, rippling muscles and taut stomach, skin the color of bronze and that dusting of dark hair that arrowed down his middle and disappeared beneath his jeans. She noted a nasty scar on his right shoulder that hadn't been there two years ago.

"Rachel?"

"What?" She snapped her eyes back to his face.

"I believe you were about to make some sort of point?"

"Yes, I was," she said, striving for indignation. But how was she supposed to think straight with him standing there and looking like…like a woman's fantasy come to life. "Just…just forget it," she finally told him. "I need to put P.J. to bed."

"I'll do it."

"That's all right," she said, and, kneeling down, held out her arms. "Come on, sweetie. It's time to go night-night."

But P.J. didn't budge. Instead he clung to Mac's leg.

"P.J., come to Mommy," she said more sternly. Then she added, "Don't you want Mommy to read you a story and tuck you in?"

"Daddy read story," P.J. said, and continued to hold on to Mac.

Mac knelt down, looked at his son. "Hey, pardner, you need to listen to your mom. Okay?"

When P.J.'s bottom lip puckered, and tears began to well in his eyes, Rachel relented. "It's all right, Mac. You go ahead and put him down."

"How about we do it together?"

But as she listened to Mac read to P.J., watched her son drift off to sleep with his father's voice in his ears,

Rachel couldn't help but worry at how attached P.J. was becoming to Mac.

True, there had been few males in P.J.'s life. Other than her father, the only other male presence with any regularity had been Alex—and that had only been for about six months. An outgoing and friendly child, P.J. had liked Alex right from the start. If he hadn't, she never would have continued to see him. Yet P.J.'s acceptance of Alex didn't come close to his affection for Mac. She hadn't anticipated her son becoming so attached to Mac so quickly. It worried her that he had. What would happen when Mac left? Because he would leave, Rachel admitted. She'd known from the start that he wouldn't stay. His leaving her nearly destroyed her two years ago. What would his leaving do to P.J.?

"I think he's asleep," Mac whispered, breaking into her thoughts.

"Yes, he is." Rachel adjusted the blanket over him, then brushed a hand over his dark curls before she pressed a kiss to his head and exited the room with Mac.

"He was one tired little guy," Mac commented as they stood outside the door of P.J.'s room.

"He had a full day."

"Yeah, he did." Mac paused, rubbed at the back of his neck. "He's a great kid, Rachel. You've done a good job with him. I just wish I had known, so that I could have helped you. I'm sure it hasn't been easy."

"I have no regrets, Mac."

"I wish I could say the same. Rachel, I—"

"Let's not rehash the past, Mac. What's done is done." Restless, she walked over to the window on the far wall of the landing and looked out at the night sky, searched for the right words. "I'm more concerned about the future. P.J.'s future and how you affect it."

"I'm not sure what you're trying to say, but I can tell you that I intend to take financial responsibility for P.J."

He came up behind her, and even before he placed his hands on her shoulders, Rachel could feel the heat of his body, smell his scent. She braced herself against the impact he had on her senses, steeled herself not to respond when his mouth brushed against her neck.

Mac turned her to face him. And slowly, oh, so slowly, he lowered his mouth until it was only a breath away from her own and whispered, "I'd like to take responsibility for both of you, if you'll let me."

And before she could answer, he covered her mouth with his own. With the same gentleness she'd witnessed him display with P.J., he coaxed her lips apart, tasted her, encouraged her to taste him. And before she realized what she was doing, her arms were wrapped around his neck, her body pressed against him, and she was kissing him back. Suddenly aware of what was happening, Rachel froze and pushed Mac away.

"Rach? What is it?"

"Don't!" She held up her hand to stop him from reaching for her again. "Please don't touch me. I can't think straight when you touch me."

Her answer produced a grin. "That's not a problem as far as I'm concerned," he told her. "You have a similar effect on me. What do you say we not think straight together?"

"Mac, please. I'm serious. We need to talk. I didn't realize how quickly P.J.'s become attached to you."

"And I've become attached to him," he said quietly, all teasing gone from his voice and expression. "I can't see where that's a problem."

Rachel sighed. She should have seen this coming, she told herself. And perhaps she would have, had she not been so distracted by her own feelings for Mac. "The problem is what happens when you leave? How do you think that's going to affect P.J.? One day you're here, and the next you're gone. He won't understand."

"Who said I was leaving?"

"We both know that, sooner or later, you'll be going back to your SEAL team."

Something flickered in Mac's eyes but was gone so quickly Rachel wondered if she'd imagined it. Then he said, "I meant what I told you. P.J.'s my son. I intend to take responsibility for him. For both of you, if you'll let me."

The sincerity of his offer touched something deep inside her, a part of her that had once dreamed of hearing Mac say those words to her. To have him say them to her now out of duty, and not love, hurt much more than when he'd said nothing at all. "I can take care of myself," she told him. "And P.J., too, for that matter. It's not money I'm talking about. It's P.J.'s attachment to you."

"It wasn't just money that I was offering," Mac informed her.

"Please, Mac, don't embarrass yourself and insult me by offering to marry me again. Believe it or not, I have no desire to be the cause for your making such a great sacrifice."

"Don't put words in my mouth, Rachel. It wouldn't be that way, and you know it."

"What I know is that getting married was never a part of your dream, never a part of your plans. It isn't what you wanted two years ago. And it isn't what you want now."

"How do you know what my dreams are, what I want?" he fired back.

"I know that being a SEAL is your dream. It's what you've always wanted, and that having your dream means there isn't room in your life for anything or anyone else because you're determined not to be like your father—a man who, according to you, put his responsibility to his family second because he wouldn't give up being a SEAL."

"I'm not my father," he told her, his expression hardening. "I would never ask you to go through what he put my mother and us kids through. Say you'll marry me, Rachel, and I-I'll resign my commission."

"Oh, Mac," she whispered, her heart aching because he meant it. And it would be the worst possible thing he could do.

He stepped closer, cupped her face. "I give you my word, Rachel. Agree to marry me, and I'll get out of the Navy. You'll never have to worry that I'll go off on a mission one day and not come back. I'll get a regular job, be an ordinary Joe who works nine-to-five and comes home every night to you and P.J."

Rachel reached up, pressed her hand against his briefly before removing his fingers from her face. "I'm sorry, Mac. I can't. We'll work something out with visitation so that you can see P.J. But as far as you and I are concerned, it's over."

Six

"**W**ell, Commander, the tests came back pretty much as expected," Captain Hayes, the doctor at the naval hospital informed him. He pointed to the X rays. "The damage from the explosion was limited primarily to the right eardrum. The hearing loss here is the most extensive, nearly 60 percent. The left ear, however, appears to be fine."

"So what's the next step?" Mac asked.

"As I explained when we spoke the last time, it's a relatively simple procedure. We'd have to do some preadmit measures, but you'd virtually be able to come in on the morning of the surgery. I'd use a local anesthetic, perform the surgery, and after a short stay in recovery, we'd send you home. You would need someone to drive you, since your equilibrium will be affected for a day or two."

"How long before we would know if the surgery worked?"

The older man removed his glasses and polished them with his handkerchief. "It's hard to give you an exact date. But usually there should be some evidence of improvement inside of a few days." He put the glasses back on and met Mac's gaze evenly. "I'd want you to come back in a week and let me administer some tests to see if there's been any improvement."

"And if there hasn't?"

Captain Hayes sat back in his chair. "Then there's nothing we can do, unless you're interested in being fitted for a hearing aid."

"I'm not," Mac said.

"No, you indicated when you first came in that it wouldn't be an alternative."

And it wasn't. Not as far as Mac was concerned. The way he saw it, he couldn't remain a SEAL without the surgery. And even then the surgery would have to be successful. But the truth was, his remaining a SEAL was no longer an option. Despite Rachel's refusal to marry him, he was sure he was making headway. And he had no intention of giving up this battle until Rachel was his wife. That meant keeping his promise to Rachel and resigning his commission. Just the thought of doing so still left an icy knot in his gut—but it was one he would learn to live with. He wasn't the selfish bastard his father had been. He refused to pursue a livelihood that would cause Rachel to shed tears as his mother had, that would risk leaving P.J. to grow up without a father. Even now he could remember that awful sound of his mother weeping at night, of his brothers never sharing those special moments a father shares with his son. He would be there for

Rachel. He would be there to teach P.J. how to throw a baseball, how to swim.

"Commander?"

"Sorry, sir," Mac said and dragged his thoughts back to the present. "You were saying?"

"As I explained earlier, this surgery is not without risks. There's a chance that the procedure will fail. If it does, you may find your hearing unchanged or you may find it diminished further."

"I understand, sir. And I'm prepared to go through with the surgery."

"Commander, I understand your eagerness to have the surgery because of your attachment to a SEAL unit. But I would urge you to think about the consequences if the surgery isn't successful. There's more to life than the Navy."

"I know that, sir. And I have considered it."

"Very well, then. Here are the release forms I'll need you to sign. The nurse can let you know what day next week I'll be available to do the surgery."

Mac signed the papers, slid them back across the desk to the doctor, then stood. "Thank you, sir."

"Commander?"

"Yes, sir?"

"Your paperwork indicated you weren't married."

"That's right, sir," Mac replied. "I'm single. At least at the moment. I hope to change that soon."

"And your fiancée…she's in favor of you having the surgery?"

"I haven't discussed it with her."

"A word of advice then. Discuss it with her. She deserves to know what could happen."

"I'm sure Rachel would agree with my decision to have the surgery, sir," Mac explained.

Dr. Hayes arched one silver brow. "I wouldn't be so sure of that, Commander. After more than twenty years of marriage, I've learned not to assume anything where my wife is concerned. Your young lady may very well surprise you. Take my advice, Commander. Discuss it with her."

After wandering about the city for the better part of three hours, Mac had come to the conclusion that perhaps the captain was right. Maybe he should explain the situation to Rachel. She hadn't agreed to marry him—but to his way of thinking, it was only a matter of time. As Chloe had reminded him, he was a SEAL. And a SEAL didn't quit just because he met with a little opposition. He *would* convince Rachel to marry him. He refused to believe otherwise.

He wasn't afraid of the surgery or its repercussions. He expected to get his hearing back. But if he didn't, he could live with it. What wouldn't be fair, he decided, was to expect Rachel to live with it. Before he talked her into marrying him, as he firmly intended to do, she deserved to know the truth about what they would be facing. To do otherwise wouldn't be right. So he would tell her— tonight—and ask her to take a chance on him. He had to give her that choice. After all, the Navy didn't want him if he was flawed, he reasoned. Maybe Rachel wouldn't want him if he were flawed, either. The very idea filled him with dread. But there was only one way to find out, and that was to lay it on the line with Rachel. He'd tell her about the surgery, even ask her to accompany him to the hospital next week. Suddenly eager to speak with Rachel and put these nagging doubts to rest, Mac pointed his truck toward the bridge that spanned the Mississippi

River and linked the Westbank where the Naval base was located to the New Orleans area.

As he drove he hit a snag of Friday-afternoon traffic. Mac frowned as he realized that somehow between the late appointment he'd scheduled and driving around in such a reflective mood afterwards, the afternoon had slipped away. Even though it was only a little past six in the evening, it was already dark, courtesy of the impending winter that officially arrived next month. Switching lanes, he prepared to exit the bridge. With a little luck, he still might arrive in time to have dinner with Rachel, P.J. and Chloe.

Ten minutes later, when he turned his truck onto Rachel's street, relief washed through him at the sight of her car parked out front. At least she was home and not trying to avoid him, he thought. Since that night nearly a week ago when they'd kissed upstairs after putting P.J. to bed, she'd done a fairly good job of doing just that. And he hadn't pushed it because he'd sensed that she needed time to come to terms with what was happening between them. So instead of pressing his case, he'd tried to prove to her in small ways that he was not like his father. He was a man she could count on to handle the small, day-to-day things. Things like repairing her spare tire, building the bookshelves for P.J.'s room that she'd mentioned she wanted, splitting and stacking firewood for the coming winter months.

He'd done everything but tell her outright that she needn't be afraid to take a chance on him because he was here to stay. It was time he told her outright. It was also time he explained about his hearing problem and found out how she felt about it. Captain Hayes had been right. This was something he should share with the woman in his life. And he wanted Rachel to be that woman. With that thought in mind, he pulled his truck up behind Rachel's car, shut off the engine and took the stairs to the house two at a time.

For once he was pleased to discover the door unlocked. "Rachel? P.J.?" he called out as he entered the house. Since it was dinnertime, he headed for the kitchen, fully expecting to find them seated at the table. Instead, he found the kitchen empty. No pots simmered on the stove. He pressed his hand to the stove's center, and found it cold. Frowning, Mac headed for the den. "Rach?" he called out, ducking his head inside the room, only to find it empty, too.

He was about to leave and check upstairs when the sound of a woman's laughter drifted on the air. Striding across the den, he headed toward the door leading to the deck out back and spied Chloe chatting with a tuxedo-clad Alex Jenkins. Mac scowled at the sight of the other man all decked out in black tie and knew instinctively that he was here for a date with Rachel. Jealousy had Mac's hands balling into fists. Among the first things he planned to do once Rachel agreed to marry him was to have her send the doctor packing. Hopefully the man would have the good sense to take off the blinders and look in Chloe's direction when she did. But that was Chloe's problem, Mac decided. Right now he needed to find Rachel. With that intention in mind, he started to turn away before they noticed him.

"Commander!"

"Damn," Mac muttered, realizing he'd waited a fraction too long.

"Commander," Chloe called again, and waved for him to come out and join them.

For a moment Mac considered pretending he hadn't heard her, but he knew that Chloe wouldn't buy it. Seeing no alternative but to say hello and make a quick exit, he opened the door.

"Why, Commander, sugar, don't you look handsome in your uniform," Chloe began, a smile curving lips painted a bold shade of orange red. "And would you look at all these medals," she murmured huskily and proceeded to skim her fingertip over all eighteen of them.

The woman was trouble, Mac thought as he stared down at the outrageous redhead. He didn't have a doubt in his mind that the fuss she was making over him was for Alex's benefit and not because she had any interest in him. As he watched her go into action, Mac was grateful that this particular package of trouble was Alex Jenkins's to deal with—even if the good doctor didn't know it yet. It was apparent to him from the way Alex's eyes never left Chloe that he was drawn to her. Not that he could blame the other man. There was a time in his life before he'd met Rachel that he would have been drawn to Chloe, too. She was, after all, the type of woman who turned a man's head. Part of it was the outer package. The heels of her slim boots made her legs look a mile long, and the chocolate leather pants she wore looked as though they'd been painted on her. The sweater—a burst of autumn in orange and brown and green—hugged her upper torso, making the most of her curves. Her hair was a riot of loose curls that framed her pale, heart-shaped face. With gold hoops in her ears and gold bracelets stacked on both wrists, she reminded him of a gypsy. The inner package—all that bravado and passion—made Chloe Chancellor an intriguing woman who could easily get under a man's skin. From the way Alex was choking his glass, he suspected that Chloe had definitely gotten under his skin.

"Have you ever seen so many medals before?" she asked Alex.

"No," Alex said curtly, his lips tightening into a disapproving line.

"Did you know that the commander here is a Navy SEAL?" she asked Alex, and Mac had to bite back a grin because for once Chloe had no trouble remembering the correct name of his particular division.

"So you've said," Alex replied, and drank deeply from his glass.

"I for one think we're all lucky to have brave warriors like the commander here risking their lives to keep us safe," Chloe told them.

"In case you haven't noticed, our country isn't at war at the moment," Alex pointed out.

"The doc's right," Mac offered. "But we SEALs consider ourselves peacekeepers. Unfortunately, sometimes we have to fight to keep that peace."

"And it's such a noble job you do," Chloe told him.

"Thank you, ma'am," Mac said and leaning closer, he whispered, "You're laying it on a bit thick."

Chloe responded by tipping her head back and laughing, which earned her another disgruntled look from Alex.

"Chloe, aren't you going to offer the commander a drink?"

"Why, of course. I was so dazzled by you in your uniform, I completely forgot my manners," she said, feigning remorse. "What can I get you to drink, Commander? I'm having a glass of wine, and Alex is having his usual scotch. But we have a full bar."

"Thanks, ma'am, but I'll pass. I was on my way upstairs. I assume that's where I can find Rachel and P.J."

"Rachel's upstairs getting ready," Alex informed him. "She and I have plans for this evening."

Not for long, Mac thought. "Then I'll see if she needs a hand with P.J."

"She doesn't," Alex informed him, and there was no mistaking the challenge in his stance.

Chloe shot Alex a look and then said, "What he means is that P.J. isn't here, Commander. Since Rachel is going out and I have plans of my own for this evening, Rachel arranged for him to spend the night at his sitter, Brenda's, house."

"Why wasn't I told about this?" Mac demanded. He didn't like the implications at all of Rachel not needing to get home to P.J.

"I suspect Rachel didn't feel she needed to consult you on the matter," Alex advised him.

"Then I guess I'll have to remind her and everyone else that I'm P.J.'s father. That means I have a right to know what's happening with my son."

"True," Alex said, and took another swallow of his scotch. "But then, I'm sure you can see where Rachel is probably used to making decisions about P.J. on her own. After all, until you showed up here recently, she's been a single mother and has had to bear sole responsibility for her son."

"She's not alone anymore," Mac said, and from the tightening of Alex's jaw, Mac knew he'd hit the mark.

"Of course Rachel's not alone. I'm not exactly chopped liver, am I?" Chloe said and tossed back her hair. "Now if you two will put a lid on all that testosterone, I suggest we go inside. It's getting a bit nippy out here." She waited for Alex to open the door for her and then strolled inside, apparently confident the two of them would follow her.

"Alex, be a dear and freshen up my wine for me, will you?" Chloe asked, and when Mac started out of the room, she quickly stepped into his path. "Commander, sugar, now just where do you think you're going?"

"Upstairs," he said curtly. Then more softly he said, "I need to speak to Rachel about something."

"Now might not be the best time," she said pointedly, and Mac didn't miss the empathy in her eyes. "Why don't I go see what's keeping her?"

"What's keeping me is the blasted zipper on the back of this dress," Rachel muttered when Chloe came upstairs to find her. "I don't know how I let you talk me into buying this thing. Besides being too expensive, it's impossible to get dressed in the thing without help."

"Quit complaining and turn around," Chloe told her, and deftly maneuvered the hidden zipper and hook. "There. Look in the mirror," Chloe commanded, and positioned her so that she was facing the old-fashioned cheval mirror.

Rachel blinked at her own reflection. The simple lines of the strapless taffeta gown did wonderful things for her figure, hinting at a tiny waist and cleavage that she didn't recall having. And the unique shade—a deep sapphire shot through with silver—made her skin seem luminous, her eyes a more intense gray. Chloe had been right about her wearing her hair up, Rachel admitted as she studied her image. The classic French twist left her neck and shoulders bare.

"That's why you let me talk you into the dress," Chloe reminded her. "You look beautiful, Rachel. Mac's going to swallow his tongue when he sees you."

"Mac's here?" Rachel asked, and could have kicked

herself for the eagerness in her voice. "I mean he's been gone all day, and I didn't realize he was back."

"Well, he is. And looking mighty handsome all dressed up in his uniform, too."

Rachel feigned indifference as she smoothed a nonexistent stray hair while a knot fisted in her stomach. Even though she'd known that Mac would be leaving eventually, and had even told herself she wanted him to go, the idea that he might soon be gone left an ache inside her. "I suppose I'd better go tell him that P.J.'s spending the night at Brenda's."

"He already knows," Chloe informed her. "Alex told him."

And Rachel could imagine how that had gone over. "I see."

"I wonder if you do, Rachel."

Rachel paused, met her friend's eyes in the mirror. "What do you mean?"

"I mean after watching you and Mac these past couple of weeks, it's pretty obvious that there's still something between you two."

"You're wrong, Chlo. I'll admit I care about him. After all, he's P.J.'s father. But whatever we had is over."

"Honey, I hate to burst your bubble but I don't think you're over the man any more than he's over you."

"You know what I think? I think that romantic streak of yours has got you seeing things that aren't there," Rachel countered. "My relationship with Mac is history. We've both moved on with our lives." Or at least she was trying to, Rachel added silently.

"Maybe you've moved on," Chloe informed her. "But I can assure you that your commander has *not* moved on. In fact, from what I just witnessed downstairs a few minutes ago, I'd say he's under the impression that there's a great deal more between the two of you than just P.J.''

Rachel's heart raced. "What are you talking about?"

"I'm talking about all the testosterone that was flying downstairs before I came up here to get you. I had to practically throw myself in front of your commander in order to keep him from taking Alex's head off."

"Mac was going to attack Alex? But why?"

Chloe shook her head. "Rachel, have you heard a word I've said? The man isn't anywhere near being over you. And if you're honest with yourself, you'll admit that you're not over him, either."

Was Chloe right? she wondered. Had she only been kidding herself that she was over Mac?

"I'm glad you have the good sense not to argue."

"Would it do me any good?" Rachel asked.

"No." She slicked on another coat of lipstick, then turned from the mirror to face her. "I know we're both pressed for time, but before we go downstairs, there is one more thing I need to get off my chest, Rach, and then I swear I'll shut up. All right?"

Rachel nodded.

"You need to decide who and what you want. And if it is Mac you want, you need to cut Alex loose. It's not right for you to go on using him."

"But I'm not using him," Rachel defended.

"Maybe not intentionally," Chloe replied. "But you don't love him. And by continuing to see him, letting him think that he might have a future with you, well it's not fair to him. Oh, I know he's got these foolish ideas about what he wants in a wife. But he's a good man, Rachel. And he deserves to be loved for who and what he is. He's never going to find that person as long as you keep him dangling.''

And Rachel realized in that instant that Chloe was talking about herself. She could have kicked herself for not seeing it before now. Touching her friend's arm, she said, ''You're in love with him.'' When Chloe didn't deny it, she asked, ''Why didn't you tell me?''

Chloe shrugged. ''Because Alex doesn't see me that way. Besides, until Mac showed up I wasn't all that sure that you didn't love Alex. I hoped you didn't,'' she admitted with a grin. ''But I wasn't sure if it was wishful thinking or not. But I'm right, aren't I? You don't love Alex.''

''No. I don't love him.'' And Rachel realized she never would.

At the sound of the doorbell Chloe said, ''That must be Derek. Come on, we'd better get downstairs.''

''Chlo, wait!''

''What?'' she countered, pausing at the door.

''If you're in love with Alex, why on earth are you going out with Derek Smallwood? You know how much Alex dislikes him.''

''Exactly,'' Chloe told her, and the grin she gave her was filled with sass.

Rachel laughed. ''You're a wicked woman, Chloe Chancellor.''

''I know,'' she said, her eyes sparking with mischief. ''Now, come on. I can't wait to see the commander's eyes roll back in his head when he gets a load of you in that dress.''

Mac's eyes didn't roll back in his head. But it was close enough, Rachel decided as she entered the den. The glass in his hand froze midway to his mouth. And his eyes… For the first time in her life Rachel thought she actually understood what it meant to be devoured by a look. Her skin felt scorched by the way those blue eyes watched her so intently. And heaven help her but she drank in the sight of him in his uniform. She didn't think it was possible for him to look more handsome than he had two years ago, yet he did.

"You look lovely," Alex told her.

"I…thank you," Rachel murmured, and yanked her gaze from Mac to Alex. Guilt prickled at her as she realized that she hadn't even noticed Alex when she'd come into the room. Her entire focus had been on Mac. No wonder Chloe had been so sure that she didn't love Alex. If she hadn't been so afraid to trust her own feelings, perhaps she would have seen it for herself. But Chloe was right. While she liked Alex and enjoyed his company, she didn't love him. And Alex deserved better.

Chloe came bustling into the room and introduced Derek to Mac. "You guys should see Derek's Harley. It's a beauty."

"So are you, doll," the twice-divorced playboy told her, and ran an appreciative gaze over Chloe. He strutted across the room toward Chloe in his black leather pants, jacket and boots and put a possessive arm around Chloe's waist. "You all set to party?"

"All set," Chloe told him.

"Then, my chariot awaits."

"Chloe, I hope you have enough sense not to go traipsing about on the back of a motorcycle," Alex told her.

"Don't worry, Doc, I've got an extra helmet for her. See you guys around."

"I don't know what Chloe sees in that idiot," Alex muttered, and Rachel didn't miss the scowl on his face as the other couple left. "Everyone knows how reckless Derek is."

"You know Chloe," Rachel told him. "She always sees the good in people."

"Yeah, well what she needs is a man who isn't dazzled by all that flash of hers to take her in hand. She's a smart and talented woman. It's time she stopped playing around and settled down."

Rachel had to bite the inside of her cheek to keep from asking Alex if he was referring to himself. "Who knows? Maybe Derek Smallwood is the man for her."

"Hardly," Alex said, his voice filled with disdain. "He's not even in Chloe's league."

"I hate to interrupt this fascinating conversation about Chloe," Mac began. "But I need to speak with Rachel for a minute?"

Rachel's pulse jumped as she met Mac's gaze, saw that heat as he watched her. Suddenly nervous, she said, "Mac, if this is about P.J. and my having him spend the night at Brenda's, I'm sorry I didn't tell you. But you were gone all afternoon."

"I know. This isn't about P.J. Not entirely. It's about us." He shot an impatient glance at Alex. "Can I speak with you alone?"

Alex stepped forward. "I'm afraid whatever's on your mind is going to have to wait, McKenna. Rachel and I have plans for the evening."

"He's right," Rachel chimed in before Mac could object. She touched his arm, felt the jolt go through them both and quickly withdrew her hand. "This isn't a good time. Alex is receiving an award tonight and we really do have to go. Can this wait until later?"

After a lengthy silence Mac said, "All right."

Alex draped her wrap around her shoulders. "Ready?"

"Yes," Rachel whispered. "Good night, Mac."

He nodded.

"Oh, McKenna," Alex added as he led her from the room, "You needn't bother to wait up for us."

Seven

"This night certainly hasn't turned out the way I expected," Alex told her as they stood on the Moonwalk in the French Quarter and stared out at the dark waters of the Mississippi River.

"I'm sorry, Alex," Rachel said, and meant it. While she would like to blame her distracted mood on her conversation with Chloe, the truth was it had been Mac who had occupied her thoughts all evening. Try as she might, she couldn't erase that image of him looking so serious, the worry she read in his eyes. "I know this was a special night for you, receiving that Humanitarian Award. You deserved better company. You should have gone with your friends to celebrate like they wanted you to. I could have taken a taxi home."

"First off, Ms. Grant, there was nothing wrong with your company. You were as lovely and charming as ever," he assured her. "Secondly, I'd rather spend time with you than waste it kicking back drinks with a bunch of what Chloe would call stuffed shirts.''

And that's just how Chloe would have described the entire affair, Rachel thought, smiling at the image of Chloe stuck in a room filled with well-meaning but pompous individuals.

"And third, my mother told me that a gentleman always returns a lady safely to her home after she's graciously agreed to go out with him for the evening.''

"Even when that lady is about as much fun as a toothache?''

Alex laughed. The sound was carefree and young, Rachel thought. And she realized that she seldom heard him laugh. In fact, for the most part, Alex seldom displayed any range of emotions with her. On the other hand, with Chloe she'd seen the man run the gamut from laughter to exasperation to anger.

"Didn't you know? Awards banquets aren't supposed to be fun.''

"You're just being nice.''

"Maybe a little,'' he confessed. "What I meant when I said things didn't turn out as I'd expected tonight, I was referring to the fact that I had planned to suggest we go for a carriage ride around Jackson Square, during which time I had planned to propose to you.''

"Oh, Alex,'' Rachel said, realizing that Chloe had been right, she had been unfair to Alex, she burst into tears. "I'm sorry. I'm so sorry. I never realized. I…I can't marry you.'' She finally got out the words and unleashed another wave of tears.

He let her cry, listened to her fumbled apology and never said a word when she told him she didn't love him. When the worst of it was over, he handed her his handkerchief. "Better?'' he asked.

''Yes,'' she said with a sniffle. ''Thank you.''

When she offered him his handkerchief back, he curled her fist around it and said, ''Keep it.''

''You must think I'm an awful person,'' she told him.

''Quite the contrary. I think you're a remarkable woman. I suspect that's why I didn't realize until tonight that I wanted to marry you for all the wrong reasons and not for the most important right one. I don't love you.''

''You don't?''

''Nope.''

Relief flooded through Rachel. ''But that's wonderful,'' she told him, and threw her arms around Alex and hugged him.

Laughing he patted her back and when they separated, he said, ''Now that we've got that out of the way, I should tell you that I also realized what or rather who my problem is. I know how I plan to deal with her. But what about you? What are you going to do about your commander?'' He frowned. ''You are in love with him, aren't you?''

The wind kicked at the water that stretched out before them, sending it crashing against the rocks below. She shoved at the strands of hair that had worked free to dance about her face. ''Yes, I'm in love with him,'' she admitted, seeing no point in continuing to deny it to herself or to Alex.

''He doesn't have a clue, does he?''

Rachel shook her head. ''And I have no intention of telling him, either.''

''Do you mind if I ask why? It's obvious he has feelings for you.''

''He feels a responsibility toward me because of P.J.,'' she explained, and when Alex arched a brow, she sighed.

"And he wants me—physically. But Mac doesn't love me."

"Are you sure? There was a moment tonight when I half expected him to come at me with his fists. And when you left with me, I almost felt sorry for the guy, he looked so lost. Desire doesn't make a guy so crazy with jealousy that he wants to break his rival in two. And desire doesn't kick the life out of a man when he thinks he's lost the woman he wants. To elicit those kind of reactions, there has to be strong feelings involved."

"Mac's just not used to losing," Rachel offered.

"You could be selling him and yourself short. Maybe you ought to give him a chance."

"It wouldn't work, Mac and I. It would be a mistake," Rachel explained. A mistake she couldn't afford to make—not and keep her fragile heart in one piece. "If there's one thing I learned the last time Mac and I were together it's that it takes more than good sex to make a relationship work."

"Since our own relationship never got that far, I'll have to take your word for it," Alex replied, a smile in his voice. "You ready to go home?"

She nodded. "Thanks, Alex. For being so understanding."

"Anytime," he told her, and led her down the steps to the street. "This has certainly been one hell of an evening. I discover that I don't love the woman I thought I wanted to marry and that she doesn't love me."

"You don't sound disappointed."

"Actually, I'm relieved," Alex confessed as he retrieved his car and opened the passenger door for her.

"So who is she?"

"She?" he asked.

"The woman you're in love with."

Alex grimaced as he pulled the car out into traffic. "You'll think I'm insane if I tell you."

"Try me."

"Chloe. Can you believe it? I can't be in the room with the woman for more than five minutes without us sniping at each other. But there you have it, I think I'm in love with her."

"I don't think it's insane at all. You two have known each other a long time."

"And we've spent most of it fighting," he added.

"Maybe all that sparring has been for a reason—because you were attracted to each other."

"Since when did you become a blond Dear Abby?" he teased.

"You forget, I know you both pretty well. I just don't know why I didn't see it before now. At any rate, congratulations."

"Don't you mean condolences?" he countered. "Even if you're right and Chloe's interested, and I'm not at all convinced she is, can you imagine what my life would be like with Chloe as a partner?"

"Fun? Interesting? Unpredictable?"

He laughed. So did she. "She'll probably spit in my face when I ask her to marry me?"

"Oh, I wouldn't be so sure about that. But there's only one way to find out," Rachel replied, and took pleasure in knowing that her friend's dream was going to come true.

"You've got a real cruel streak in you, Ms. Grant. I think I'm going to enjoy watching you make the commander suffer."

Rachel chose not to respond. After all, she reasoned, she had no intention of making Mac suffer—not that she could. Despite what Alex might think, Mac wasn't in love with her.

"Well, well, now. Looks like he decided to wait up for you after all."

"What?" Rachel replied, and realized that he had turned the corner onto her street.

"Your commander," Alex explained as he headed toward the house. "I suspect that's him I see wearing out the boards on your porch."

Rachel looked toward the end of the block and spied the movement on the porch. And the nerves came back in droves.

"Forgive me, Rachel. But one good turn deserves another. I think it's time I gave your commander a little wake-up call."

"A wake-up call? Alex, what are you going to do?" Rachel asked, anxious.

"Up the ante."

Just how long does it take to eat a cardboard-chicken dinner? Mac wondered as he paced the length of the veranda and waited for Rachel to return home. He looked at his watch for the fifth time in as many minutes and scowled at the hands indicating it was nearly midnight.

Frustrated, Mac slapped his hands against the door. He closed his eyes, tried to shut off his brain and not imagine Rachel with Alex. To do so only tied him up in knots. At the sound of a car door slamming, Mac spun around.

"Damn," he muttered. He hadn't even heard the car approach. Iron Mike had been right. He was no good to the SEAL team like this. His hearing problem made him dead weight. If the surgery didn't work, they would have had to cut him loose. Not that it mattered now, he told himself. It didn't since he'd already made up his mind to resign his commission.

And while his hearing might be less than perfect, there wasn't a damn thing wrong with his eyesight, Mac thought as he watched Rachel approach. Her hair looked mussed, her eyes bright. Imagining Alex running his fingers through her hair, whispering things in her ear, his blood chilled. As the other man came into view, Mac noted that he'd shed his tie and had opened the collar of his shirt. And the chill in his veins turned into white-hot fury.

"Mac," Rachel said, her voice breathless as she paused to look up at him from the bottom step of the porch. "What are you doing out here at this time of night?"

"Waiting for you," he said between gritted teeth.

"That was nice of you, Commander, but you'll recall I told you that you shouldn't wait up for us."

Mac curled his hands into fists at his sides to keep from going for the guy's throat. "We need to talk, Rachel."

"I, um, yes. Why don't you go on inside. I'll be there in a moment."

Mac didn't budge.

Alex chuckled. "Darling, I don't believe the commander trusts me alone with you. Is that right, Commander?"

"You got it, ace."

"Mac, you're embarrassing me," Rachel told him. "I said I'd be inside in a moment. I want to say good-night to Alex."

Mac folded his arms across his chest and maintained his stance. "I prefer waiting here. But you go ahead and say goodbye to the doctor," Mac suggested. Because he'd made up his mind. If the fancy doctor so much as pecked Rachel on the cheek, the man was dead meat.

Rachel shot him a quelling glance before turning to face Alex. "I had a lovely time this evening," she told him.

"So did I," Alex said, a smile on his face as he took Rachel's hand and kissed it. "Don't forget what we talked about."

"I won't," Rachel murmured. "Thanks again."

And while Mac had been prepared to break the other man into pieces if he kissed Rachel, he could only stand there feeling helpless and furious as Rachel reached up and pressed a kiss to the doctor's mouth. It was over in the blink of an eye, but seeing Rachel kiss another man was like a kick in the gut.

"Good night, darling. I'll give you a call in the morning and set up a time for us to go look at rings."

"The hell you will," Mac fired back and came off the porch in a flash. "The only ring she's going to be wearing is mine."

"How dare you?" Rachel demanded, blocking his path. "Just who do you think you are, Mac McKenna?"

"I'm the man you're going to marry," he informed her, and he realized in that moment that he truly meant it.

"The hell I will." Rachel tossed his words back at him.

"Doesn't sound to me like the lady is too keen on the idea, Commander."

"You stay out of this."

"I'm afraid I can't do that, Commander. You see I'm very fond of Rachel. I couldn't possibly let her marry someone like you. She'd be much better off with a gentleman."

"Someone like you?" Mac countered.

"As a matter of fact, yes."

"We'll see just how a gentleman like you feels with my fist planted in your face," Mac fired back, eager to wipe that smug look off the doc's face. "Get out of my way, Rachel."

"No."

"Fine, have it your way," Mac told her and catching her by the waist, he prepared to set her aside.

Rachel wrapped her arms around his neck. "Mac, stop it," she commanded. "You're making a fool of yourself."

"And a brilliant job he's doing of it, too," Alex added.

"Damn it, Rachel. Let me go so I can pound that prissy face of his in!"

"No."

Seeing no alternative, he scooped her up into his arms. At that moment lights flickered on inside the house and the front door opened. Out came a sleepy-eyed Chloe wearing a T-shirt that barely covered her rear and boasted 'Bikers Make Better Lovers'. The T-shirt drooped dangerously on one shoulder. "Do you guys have any idea what time it is? Some of us are trying to sleep."

"Chloe," Alex said her name and the amused look disappeared from his face. "I...you...you're home."

"Of course I'm home. I live here, remember? Besides where else would I be?"

"I...I...no reason. No reason at all. It's just that I thought..."

"Mac, put me down," Rachel demanded.

"Not a chance, sweetheart." He took another look at the doc who was standing there stammering and gaping at Chloe like a fish caught on a hook. Then he looked at the squirming female he held in his arms. Deciding he had what he wanted, he headed toward the door. "Excuse me, ma'am," he told Chloe.

As Chloe stepped aside, the lights flickered on next door. "Chloe? Rachel? Is that you two girls I hear?"

"Oh, my God, now you've done it. You've woken up Mrs. Brezinsky." Groaning, Rachel buried her face in his shoulder.

"Aw, hell," Chloe muttered. "Now the whole neighborhood's going to hear about this."

"Chloe?" Mrs. Brezinsky called out again, and the screen door opened.

"For heaven's sake, Mac, hurry up and get me inside," Rachel ordered.

"Whatever you say, ma'am," he told her and zipped inside the house.

"You can put me down now."

If Mac heard her, he gave no indication. His expression remained stony as he continued through the house with her in his arms. Two years ago, during the time they had been together, she would have sworn she had witnessed all of Mac's moods—proud and serious when he spoke of his work as a SEAL, brave and considerate when dealing with others, playful, loving and tender with her. But always, even when he faced danger as he had during that rescue, he had retained rigid control over his emotions.

Until tonight.

Tonight Mac had displayed none of that steely control that she had alternately admired, envied and even hated. Tonight he had been the prime example of a jealous man. So jealous that he had even threatened Alex with violence. It didn't make any sense to her. But then, neither did the angry determination she sensed in him now.

She'd assumed he was delivering her to the den. But

when he turned the corner and started up the stairs, Rachel's heartbeat quickened. While she wasn't afraid of Mac and knew he would never force her to do anything against her will, she didn't see the point in tempting them both. Trying again, she said, "I'm quite capable of walking up the stairs on my own, and I'd appreciate it if you would put me down. Now."

Her imperious tone was met with more silence. Without breaking stride or so much as breathing hard, he made his way up the long, curving staircase in nothing flat, then headed toward her bedroom. "I thought you wanted to talk," Rachel accused, suddenly nervous at the prospect of being alone in a bedroom with Mac.

He stopped in front of her bedroom door and finally he looked at her. "I do want to talk. And we're going to talk," he assured her.

The determination she read in those deep-blue eyes had her stomach tightening again—only to dip as he opened the door. "Mac, this isn't a good idea."

He swept a glance around the room, then walked over to the bed at the room's center and placed her atop it. Then, without saying a word, he headed back toward the door.

Rachel started to release a breath she hadn't even realized she'd been holding when he flipped the lock. Dumbfounded, it took her a full moment to gather her wits and scramble off the bed. "Just what do you think you're doing?" she demanded, surprised that she could sound so in command of herself when her heart was racing like a freight train.

"I should think it would be obvious," he said calmly, and started back toward her. "I'm ensuring that we have some privacy for once. You and I are going to talk, Rachel Grant. And this time we're actually going to finish the conversation without being interrupted.''

"Fine. You want to talk? We'll talk. But we'll do it downstairs."

When she attempted to move past him, he stepped into her path. "We go downstairs, and there's a pretty good chance that I'll have to plant my fists in your pal Alex's pretty face. Since I doubt that you'll feel kindly toward me once I do that, I suggest we stay here."

Exasperated, Rachel crossed her arms and met his cool gaze. "Fine. Then let's get this over with. What is it you're so anxious to tell me?"

"Several things. But we'll start with the good doctor downstairs."

"What about Alex?"

He moved a step closer so that the toes of his boots nudged the toes of her peau de soie pumps. "You're not going to marry him."

"Is that so?"

"Yes, that's so."

Even though she'd already come to the same conclusion, his high-handed manner sent her temper soaring. She hiked up her chin. "And give me one good reason why I should listen to you?"

"I'll give you three. First," he said, ticking off his finger. "You don't love him. Second, I think you're still in love with me. And third," he ticked off that third digit. "There's only one man I intend to let you marry and that's me."

"That's quite a speech, Commander. Unfortunately, you're wrong on all counts," she fibbed and had the satisfaction of seeing him flinch. "Now if you'll excuse me, I'd better go check on Chloe. She—"

He caught her by the shoulders, pulled her close, and

Rachel swallowed at the wild panic in those blue eyes. "You don't love him. If you did you could never have responded to me the way you did when I kissed you."

With an aplomb foreign to her, she countered, "You're a skilled lover, Mac. It's only natural that I—"

He made some sound deep in his throat, part groan, part plea and then he took her mouth. There was no seductive teasing this time, no gentle coaxing. Instead there was only need. A need that bordered on desperation, that burned and consumed with the intensity of emotion behind it.

Rachel could no more turn him away than she could stop herself from drawing her next breath. She slid her arms up his chest, roped them around his neck and gave herself to him in the kiss.

When he lifted his head, his breathing was raspy, his eyes hot and reflecting the same panic she'd tasted in his kiss. He cupped her face, stared at her the way a man trapped in a desert stares at a glass of water. "You're not going to marry him," he told her.

She turned her face into his hand and pressed a kiss into his palm. "No, I'm not going to marry Alex."

"Because you don't love him."

She looked up at him, saw the triumph mingled with hope in his eyes. "Because I don't love him," she repeated.

"Say the rest, Rachel. Say that you love me. You told me you did once. Tell me again now."

She did love him, but self-preservation and the scars from two years ago kept the words locked inside her heart now. Instead she took his hand and led him to the bed where she tried to show him with her mouth as she kissed his face, his lips, eased open the buttons of his denim shirt and tasted his bare flesh. And she tried to show him with her hands as she reached for his belt buckle and unsnapped his jeans. When she slid down the zipper and cupped his straining manhood, Mac groaned.

He speared his fingers through her hair, sent pins scattering as he drew her face to him. Then Mac was the one kissing her. Her eyes. The lobe of her ear. The corner of her mouth, her chin. He worked his way down, kissing and tasting her neck, her throat, her bare shoulders, the tender skin where the strapless gown dipped at her breasts. So caught up was she in the feel of his mouth that Rachel didn't even feel the release of the zipper on her gown until it puddled about her feet. She stepped out of it, kicked it aside. Feeling exposed, vulnerable, she used her hands to cover the black strap of lace that lifted her breasts.

"Don't," Mac said, his voice tender, his eyes hot. "Let me see you." Gently he removed her hands. His eyes darkened as he looked at her and when he lifted his gaze to hers, he whispered, "You're so beautiful. More beautiful than I remembered. And I did remember. There hasn't been a day that's gone by in more than two years that I haven't closed my eyes and seen you. I've missed you, Rachel."

Something inside her shifted, swelled. "Show me," she told him.

And he did.

He released the catch at the center of her bra, bared her breasts to his eyes, to his touch, to his mouth. When he took one nipple into his mouth, grazed it with his teeth, Rachel cried out, "Mac!"

Were it not for the fact that she was leaning against the bed, Rachel was sure her knees would have buckled from the sensations rolling through her. Closing her eyes, she clutched at the bedding, curled her fists into the folds of the comforter and sheets as Mac ministered to her other breast. And then he moved lower—tasting, exploring her midriff, her navel, the pale skin of her belly. She could feel every stroke of his tongue, every nip of his teeth, every stubble of the five o'clock shadow that darkened his chin. And as his mouth continued its tender assault to her senses, her body burned even hotter. She ached for even more.

Mac caught the tiny piece of black lace that covered her femininity and slipped it off, leaving her naked save for the sheer black hose with the scalloped lace tops that ended at her thighs, and the high-heel pumps.

He lifted his head, looked up at her out of fevered eyes. ''You look like a pagan goddess,'' he murmured.

While she was still reeling from the pleasure of his words, he lowered his head once more and pressed his mouth to her center. Rachel gasped. And when she would have pulled away, he whispered, ''Please. Let me love you.''

And he did love her, using his tongue, his teeth, his lips.

Her body was on fire and she could barely breathe as his mouth continued its tender assault. When the first spasm hit her, sent pleasure flooding through her, she fisted her hands in his hair and cried out his name.

She'd barely caught her breath when he replaced his mouth with his fingers and sent her up and flying again. ''Mac, please,'' she pleaded, reaching for him, seeking his mouth, needing to show him that she loved him even as she held back the words.

''I wanted to go slow, to make this special for you,'' he whispered against her lips. ''But I want you too badly. I can't wait, Rach.''

"Then don't," she told him as she freed him and closed her fingers around him.

"Rachel," he cried out her name.

When he fumbled with the foil packet, she took it from him and ripped it open with her teeth. Then she slid the protection over his hard length. And with a boldness that shocked her, she guided him to her center.

Mac made some animal sound deep in his throat and then he reached for her. Anchoring his hands at her hips, he slid himself home.

Rachel sucked in a breath. And then he began to move inside her, each stroke deeper, harder, faster than the one before until a new storm was building inside her—bigger, stronger, more dangerous than the before. The sound of his quickened breathing and the naked hunger in his eyes fed the desire racing through her veins and pushed aside the loneliness she'd lived with since he'd made love to her last. Clutching his shoulders, she scored him with her nails and bit down on her lip to keep from telling him she loved him. When he thrust into her again, pushed her closer to the edge of that storm, Rachel arched her back like a bow.

"Open your eyes, Rachel," he said, his voice part command, part plea. "I want...I need to see you when I make you mine again."

So she opened her eyes, saw her own need reflected in his. And when he drove into her again, when the first wave of that storm hit, she forced herself to hold his gaze, saw his triumph when the first shudder ran through her.

"Mine," he called out. "You're mine."

Even as the sensations pulled her under, tossed her about a raging sea, she held on to him, dragged him into the storm-tossed waters with her. And when she heard him cry out her name and follow her into the swirling waters, she echoed his words, "Mine. You're mine."

And then Rachel could no longer think. All she could do was feel as she and Mac, joined together as one, dove even deeper into the endless storm.

Eight

Mac came awake as he always did—instantly and fully alert. Depending on his perspective, it was either one of the benefits or curses of his SEAL training. Either way, he had long ago grown accustomed to getting by on short amounts of sleep. Now he seldom found himself able to sleep through the night.

Not that he had actually done much sleeping, he recalled with a smile. After that first frantic session of love-making, he and Rachel had made love a second time before falling into an exhausted sleep. He glanced at the woman curled up beside him. Although dawn was still hours away, he had no trouble seeing her in the dark. He'd told her that she'd looked like a pagan goddess last night when she'd stood beside the bed wearing next to nothing, her hair a tumbled mass of blond silk. Yet now, with just a plain cotton sheet draped across her body and her eyes closed in slumber, he found her even more arresting. Giving in to the urge, he pressed a kiss to the top of her head. She made some mewling sound, snuggled closer and sent desire stirring in his blood once more. Part Madonna, part siren, Mac thought with a sigh, wanting her again.

And as he watched her, wanted her, he could feel that tightening in his chest again, that yearning for something more than the physical, something deeper. The emotional need disturbed him, Mac admitted. He was familiar with desire, knew how to handle it. It was the emotions—this mixture of longing and fear inside him—that he didn't know how to deal with, didn't know how to control.

And it was that inability to control his emotions where Rachel was concerned that he feared the most. He wanted her and he wanted P.J. and he intended to have them both, Mac acknowledged as he eased his arm from around her so that he could lie back and stare up at the ceiling. He thought about the surgery, resigned himself to the fact that its success and his being able to remain a SEAL had been a long shot at best and one not without risk. But with a son and soon a wife, remaining a SEAL was no longer an option for him. So he saw no point in going forward with the surgery.

In the morning he would tell Rachel about his hearing loss. And while the SEALs would not want him in his damaged state, Rachel would. Any doubts he had that she might no longer love him had been answered last night when she'd taken him to her bed.

As though she sensed his heavy thoughts, Rachel stirred beside him, and the movement caused the sheet to slide, baring her shoulder and the top of her breasts. He shouldn't want her again so soon, Mac told himself. Yet he did. Already hard and aching for her, he squeezed his eyes shut to block out the tempting sight and reminded himself that Rachel needed to rest even if he didn't.

But closing his eyes did little to ease his hunger for her. How could it when he could feel her soft skin pressed against him. When he could smell that faint rose scent she wore. When he could all too clearly recall the taste of her in his mouth. Even now he could still hear the sound of his name on her lips as she came apart with him buried deep inside her.

Damn! When had wanting Rachel become an all-encompassing need?

"Mac?" She touched his shoulder. "Mac, what's wrong?"

Mac snapped open his eyes. "I'm sorry, I didn't mean to wake you."

Shifting up on one elbow, he drank in the sight of her clutching the sheet to her breasts, her hair all mussed and falling in thick waves past her shoulders. Her eyes still held the softness of sleep. But her mouth—that oh-so-wonderful mouth—was too tempting to ignore. Gently he kissed her. And when he lifted his head, he said, "I really am sorry. I never meant to wake you."

"It's all right. What time is it?" she asked, and then yawned.

"A little past four in the morning."

She groaned. "I forgot that, unlike us mere mortals, you need very little sleep to function," she said, and rested her head against his shoulder.

"Hey, we can't all be superheroes," he told her, and bit back a grimace as she slid her arm across his middle. When she settled one of her legs between his, sweat beaded across his brow with the effort it took not to give in to the urge to turn and bury himself inside her yet again. "Go on back to sleep," he said, and resigned himself to the torture of just holding her.

"What about you?"

"I'm fine," he lied.

She slid her hand down his belly, then lower and, discovering his state of arousal, she lifted her gaze to his. "Now I understand the reason you're so tense. Why don't I see if I can help you relax a bit," she murmured, and began pressing open-mouthed kisses to his chest.

"Um, Rachel darling," he said, his voice strained. "Trust me, that is *not* going to help me relax."

"No?" She glanced up at him for a moment with devilment in her eyes before she pushed aside the sheet covering him and resumed making a trail down his chest to his stomach with her mouth.

Mac nearly came off the bed when her tongue circled the tip of his shaft.

"You're right," she said, laughing. "This doesn't seem to be helping you relax. Want me to stop?"

Mac grunted.

At his response, she laughed and said, "I'll take that as a no."

How on earth had he managed to get by without hearing that laugh for more than two years? Simple, he had only been half-alive, he concluded, and then all semblance of thought left his head as she took him into her mouth.

A few minutes later when he was sure he would go insane from the pleasure and desire building inside him, she replaced her mouth with her body and sent all thoughts but one from his head: Rachel and the need to make her his—physically, emotionally, all ways. She straddled him. And as she lowered herself onto his shaft, Mac held on to her hips. Then she began to move.

The slow, sweet rhythm was exquisite. So was allowing Rachel to take control. She was magnificent as she rode him and brought them both closer and closer to the brink. When the first spasm hit her, she shuddered and cried out his name. And as he watched the pleasure take her, send her up and over the waves, he fought back his own release and urged her on. Finally, when he could wait no longer, Mac flipped Rachel so that she was beneath him. Linking their hands together, he drove into her again and again, faster and faster still. When Rachel cried out his name again, Mac felt his world explode.

Later as she lay in his arms with her head against his heart, her body still tangled with his, and slept, Mac snuggled her closer. And as the first rays of dawn began to creep through the window, he realized that for the first time in over two years he felt whole again.

"It smells fabulous," Rachel told Mac as she sat at the table in the kitchen later that morning. Her mouth watered as he piled several strips of bacon next to the silver-dollar pancakes, eggs and buttered toast. Noticing that he hadn't served anything for himself, she asked, "Aren't you going to eat?"

"I already did...two hours ago."

Rachel flushed. "I don't usually sleep this late."

He poured himself a cup of coffee, then straddled the chair next to her. "That's because I suspect that you usually sleep when you go to bed. Last night you didn't," he reminded her, a satisfied grin on his lips.

Deciding it best not to respond, she took a bite of the pancakes drenched in cane syrup and moaned.

Mac laughed. "Does that mean you like it?"

"It means I think I've died and gone to heaven. I can't remember the last time I had pancakes that tasted this good.'' She broke off a piece of the bacon with her fingers. ''Chloe would kill for a home-cooked breakfast like this. I really should go wake her up and share this.''

''She's not here,'' Mac told her as he swiped a slice of her toast and devoured it in two bites.

Rachel paused with her coffee cup midair. ''Of course she's here. Chloe never gets up before eleven.''

''Car's gone.''

Catching him eyeing a strip of her bacon, Rachel took the empty plate in the table setting on the other side of her, divvied up the breakfast feast and slid it in front of Mac.

''Thanks,'' he said with a smile. ''I guess I worked up an appetite again fixing this.''

''Looks that way.''

He polished off a slice of the bacon. ''My guess is she's with Jenkins.''

Rachel thought about it, hoped Mac was right. Sitting here with Mac this way after the night they had spent together, she found it hard to grasp that in the past twenty-four hours her entire life seemed to have been turned upside down.

''You okay about it?'' he asked.

''About what?''

''About Chloe and Jenkins.''

Rachel tilted her head, realized the intensity of Mac's expression. ''Why wouldn't I be?''

''Chloe told me that the two of you had been seeing each other for the past six months,'' he confessed, his voice hard, his expression grim. ''Things sounded kind of serious between you two last night before I... before...''

Enjoying herself, Rachel said, ''Before you pulled

your caveman stunt and carried me upstairs and made wild, passionate love to me?''

He caught her fingers, squeezed them in his. ''I nearly went nuts imagining you with him. When you kissed him, I...I guess I lost it.''

''Oh, Mac. It was never that way between Alex and me. I mean he and I never, we didn't...'' She stopped, drew in a breath. ''There hasn't been anyone since you.''

''That makes two of us,'' he told her.

Rachel blinked. He couldn't possibly mean...''But it's been over two years,'' she pointed out.

''Believe me, I'm well aware of that fact.''

''But why?'' She swallowed. ''I mean, I know you've been on some hush-hush SEAL missions to God-knows-where, but surely there were women.''

''There were women. I just wasn't interested,'' he admitted. ''There hasn't been anyone since you for me either.''

Stunned and thrilled at the same time, she didn't know what to say. A dozen different thoughts whirled through her head, and the most important one was that surely Mac had remained celibate because he loved her. She desperately wanted to hear the words, had prayed when she held them back last night that Mac would say them to her. Only he hadn't. Nor had he said them early this morning when he'd made love with her again.

''Since you're not eating, should I assume you're finished with your breakfast?''

She yanked her thoughts back to the present and realized that she'd forgotten all about her breakfast. She glanced down at the food she was so ravenous for only a few moments ago, then back up at Mac. ''No, you should not assume any such thing. I'm still working on it,'' she told him and forked up a bite of egg to prove her point. Then she saw his empty plate and it dawned on her that he might want more. "But if you're still hungry, I'll be happy to share some more of my pancakes."

"That's sweet and I appreciate the offer." He leaned over and kissed her slowly, thoroughly. "But it's not food that I'm hungry for," he whispered against her lips.

Rachel's pulse skipped at the heat in those blue eyes. When he sat back in his chair, she shifted her gaze to the front of his jeans and noted the telltale bulge. "You can't possibly be serious."

"But I *am* serious," he told her. "I want you, Rachel Grant. Right now. An hour from now. A week, a month, a year, ten years from now. I want you all the time. Even when I'm inside you, it isn't enough, because I already want you again."

The air backed up in her lungs at his declaration. Anticipation made her already-fast-beating heart race harder as she waited for him to finally tell her that he loved her.

"So what do you say, beautiful? Do you want to christen the kitchen or do we go back upstairs?"

Disappointment was a sharp lance to her heart and took some of her earlier joy with it. Adopting a savoir faire she didn't feel, she patted his cheek. "Sorry, sailor. I've already had my way with you. But this feast…well, there's no way I'm going to let it go to waste."

Regret shone in his eyes a moment, then he grinned and reached for his cup. "And to think my mother swore one day I'd thank her for insisting I learn how to cook."

"I didn't realize your mother was the one responsible for your talent in the kitchen. I always assumed it was one more thing they taught you during SEAL training."

"Nope. All my mom's idea."

"You never say much about her or your brothers. Other than the fact that your father was a Navy SEAL who died when you were ten, I know very little about your family. Tell me about them,'' Rachel asked.

The teasing grin of a moment ago dissolved. ''What do you want to know?''

''Whatever you want to tell me.'' Two years ago when they'd been together, he'd given her the bare bones of his family dynamics. She hadn't pressed him then because she'd sensed it wasn't something he liked talking about. ''Why don't you start by telling me where they live, what they do.''

''They all live in Texas. My mother is manager of a ritzy bed and breakfast in the Dallas/Fort Worth area. One of my brothers is a computer whiz and works for a tech company and the other one is working on his Ph.D. in physics at the University of Texas.''

She slathered more butter on a slice of toast. ''So why did your mother insist you learn how to cook?''

He hesitated for so long, Rachel thought he wasn't going to answer, then he began to explain. ''I was ten when my dad was killed. My brother Josh was five and Mick was only four. That first year…it was pretty rough on all of us. Especially on my mother. I've never known two people who loved each other the way my parents did. They were everything to each other. So when Dad was killed, it was like a part of her had been killed, too. She didn't want to go on living without him.''

''But she had you. And your brothers.''

''Yeah. If she hadn't had us kids depending on her, I'm not sure what she would have done.''

Which explained why Mac had always shied away from the word *love* as he did. For him love was associated with loss and pain, Rachel realized. ''Then I guess it's a good thing she had you and your brothers. That way she still had a part of your father.''

"I guess. Anyway, she moved us back to Texas where she had family and friends. My mom had married my dad right out of school, so she'd never had a career except to be the captain's wife and then our mother. But one day a friend of hers who worked at a small hotel called and said she was in a bind. They were short-staffed and the hotel was full. She asked if my mom would help out for the weekend."

"And your mother went and ended up landing a job," Rachel concluded.

"Not exactly, but close enough. She found out that she was good at organizing things and she was always good with people. I think going to work saved her sanity and helped her get over losing my dad some."

"So, how did that lead to your learning to cook?" Rachel asked.

Mac made a face. "Unfortunately, my mother didn't approve of us boys living on pizza and fast food. Her solution was that we boys learn to cook—or at least me at the start, since I was the oldest."

"She sounds like a very special woman."

"She is," he replied. "I think you'd like her, and I'm sure she'd adore you. And as for P.J., well, she's going to be nuts about him. She's been making noises for years about wanting grandchildren."

Rachel swallowed hard. "Does she know about P.J.?"

"Yes. I called and told her after I found out. She can't wait to meet him and you."

The statement had nerves jumping in her stomach. "So is your mother coming to New Orleans soon?"

"She's working on clearing her schedule now. With Thanksgiving only a week away, she's got to do some juggling. Finished?" he asked.

"I, um, yes. Thank you. It was delicious."

"You're welcome." He reached for her plate, stacked it atop his and started for the sink.

"Mac, I'll take care of the dishes. It's the least I can do since you cooked."

"Forget it," he said, and shot her a glance over his shoulder that had her sliding back down to her seat. "The other thing my mother taught me was to clean as I go. These plates and silverware will only take me a few seconds. You go ahead and finish your coffee."

She did as he said, mulled over his remark about his mother coming to meet her and P.J. Of course, the woman was really coming to meet her grandson, she reminded herself. But Rachel couldn't help but wonder what Mrs. McKenna would think of the woman who had borne her son's child and kept it a secret for eighteen months.

"Why such a long face?"

Rachel yanked her gaze up and realized that Mac was standing in front of her. "I...I was thinking about meeting your mother, wondering what she must think of me."

Mac stroked her cheek with fingers that were slightly damp and smelled of dish soap. Then he leaned down and pressed a gentle kiss to her lips. When he lifted his head, his eyes were dark, serious. "She'll think that I'm one lucky guy to have P.J. as my son and you as my future wife."

Rachel snapped her head back.

"I already have the ring. I bought it right after I found out about P.J. I wanted to give it to you that next day when I came over, but you wouldn't even discuss it." He dug into the pocket of his jeans and pulled out a small black jewelers' box and opened it to show her a lovely diamond solitaire set in a thin gold band. A matching wedding band sat nestled in a bed of black velvet. "I thought it looked elegant and graceful—like you."

"Oh, Mac, it's lovely, but—"

"Marry me, Rachel. I want you, P.J. and me to be a real family."

Want, Rachel thought. Not love. Never love. While she could understand now why the prospect of falling in love would scare Mac, it didn't make the fact that he wouldn't allow himself to love her any easier to accept.

"I don't want to wait any longer than we have to. So unless you have your heart set on some big, fancy wedding, I thought we'd just go ahead and have a small ceremony with your family, my mother and brothers and a few close friends. We could get married here or if you'd prefer we can go to Mississippi and be married in your father's church."

Still in shock, Rachel looked up from the hand that Mac now held and was attempting to put a ring on. She snatched her hand away. "Mac, I never said I was going to marry you."

"But last night…"

"You think last night changed things?"

All of the tenderness and joy died in his eyes. He pulled his mouth into a grim line. "Are you going to tell me that it didn't? That last night when you were crying out my name, when I was buried deep inside you, that all that meant nothing to you?"

"No. I'm not going to lie to you. It did mean a great deal to me," she admitted. "Just as you mean a great deal to me. You always did, Mac. You always will." And she knew she would go on loving him for the rest of her life even if he didn't love her. But what she wouldn't do was marry him. To do so would be a mistake for both of them.

"Then I don't see the problem. We care about each other, Rachel. You've said so yourself. And there's no question that we're compatible sexually. Plus don't forget we have a child together that binds us to each other for the rest of our lives. That's a hell of a lot more than most married people have going for them."

"But it's not enough for me."

Nine

Mac stared at the woman who only hours ago had made wild, passionate love with him. There was nothing passionate or loving about the closed, distant expression on her face now. He looked down at the ring he still held in his hand, then back up into those cool gray eyes. "You're serious," Mac said aloud, and wondered what in the hell had gone wrong. He'd been so sure that after last night Rachel would agree to marry him.

"Yes, I am serious. I'm not going to marry you, Mac."

Frustrated, Mac tossed the ring onto the table and jammed his fist through his hair. As he always did when he was restless and confused, he began to pace. "But why? Give me one good reason why you won't marry me."

She paused so long, Mac thought she wasn't going to answer him. Then she said, "Because good sex and a baby are the wrong reasons for two people to commit to spending the rest of their lives together. And that's what marriage would be for me, Mac. A lifetime commitment.''

''Don't you think I know that? I'd be making the same commitment.'' He marched back over to her and stood practically toe-to-toe, willed her to look at him. Gentling his voice, he said, ''Rach, I wouldn't be marrying you just because of P.J. and the sex. I told you, I care about you. I always have. Do you have any idea how hard it was for me to walk away from you the way I did?''

''Funny, but you didn't seem to have a hard time telling me to find someone else, that you weren't the man for me.'' Her voice broke. Tears shone in her eyes.

''Rachel, honey—''

''Don't,'' she said, and he let his hand fall to his side. After a moment she continued, ''I loved you and you broke my heart, Mac. Do you have any idea how I felt, having you tell me that you didn't want me?''

''I never said that,'' Mac countered.

''Maybe not in those exact words, but you made it clear that there wasn't room in your life for me.''

Something inside him broke at the sight of tears spilling down her cheeks. ''Rachel—''

She slapped his hand away. ''I distinctly remember the speech you gave me that night about how being a SEAL and having a wife and a family didn't mix. About how I deserved to have a husband who came home to me at night, how I deserved to have a family. How I should forget about you, find a good man, one who could offer me the things that you couldn't.''

Mac could have kicked himself as she tossed his words back at him. Only now could he see how deeply he had hurt her. ''I'm sorry,'' he murmured, and this time she allowed him to wipe away the tears that slid down her cheek. "Please don't cry, baby. I never meant to hurt you."

"But you did hurt me, Mac. And I'm not going to let you hurt me again by marrying you just to...to satisfy your need to do the honorable thing because of P.J."

"I told you P.J. is only part of the reason I asked you to marry me." He caught her hands in his and looked into her eyes. "Don't you know that I'm nuts about you? That I always have been?"

"Then why didn't you ask me to marry you two years ago?"

"Things were different then," he said and cringed at how lame he sounded.

She tugged her hands free. "What was so different? We're the same people we were then, Mac. You're still a Navy SEAL. And according to you two years ago, marriage and a family and your being a SEAL would be a disastrous mix. So what makes it work now?"

"Because I'm not going to be a SEAL. At least not much longer. I'm resigning my commission." Saying the words aloud still burned like acid on his tongue and left a hollow feeling in his stomach.

Rachel sank down into the chair, evidently shocked by his declaration. "Why? You love being a SEAL. How could you even consider giving it up?"

"Two reasons. First, I love you and I love our son and I want us to be a family." Funny, he thought, how finally saying the words, admitting that he did love her, had been so easy. "But I meant what I said about being a SEAL and having a family not working. I promised myself I'd never put anyone through what my mother and my brothers and I went through when we lost my dad." He waited a moment, hoped that his own declaration of love would enable Rachel to tell him that she loved him.

"I don't agree with your reasoning, Mac, that you have to give up the job you adore in order to have a family. But I'll save that for now. What's the second reason?"

Disappointed in her response, he answered, "Because I failed my last physical. I'm not good enough to be a SEAL anymore."

She tilted her head, stared at him with confusion in her eyes. "I don't understand. How could you not be good enough? Look at you. You're in terrific shape."

Mac washed a hand down his face. "It's my hearing. On my last mission, we had to get some people out of an American embassy that was under attack and destroy the compound to keep any sensitive documents out of enemy hands," he began.

Taking himself back to that fateful day, he continued to relate the events. "The rescue went as planned and I wired the place, set it to blow a few minutes after I knew we'd be out. Then in the chopper the ambassador's kid starting crying for her dog. They'd forgotten the fur ball in the excitement. So I went back in, got the little guy, tucked him in my jacket and ran like hell. We made it out of the compound only seconds before the place blew. But the explosion...I was too close and my ear..."

"Oh, Mac," Rachel said, and without him even realizing she had moved, her arms were wrapped around his middle. "I'm so sorry."

He closed his arms around her, breathed in her scent and took comfort in the feel of her pressed against him.

She eased herself back slightly and looked up at his face. "How bad is it?"

"My right ear took the brunt of the blast. There was some damage and I've lost about 50 percent of my hearing in that ear. So you see, my being a SEAL, it's no longer an issue. You have to be at peak physical condition to be a SEAL. Nothing less is acceptable.''

''But that seems so unfair.''

''It's the way it has to be,'' he explained, warmed by her defense of him. ''My not being able to hear, it could get me killed and endanger my team. So I'm going to go ahead and resign my commission.''

''Still, it just doesn't seem right. Are you sure there isn't anything that can be done? Maybe if you saw a specialist.''

''I've already seen several specialists. It's actually why I came to New Orleans, to see the ENT guy at the naval base here. He specializes in hearing problems like mine and has had some success reversing the damage with surgery.''

''Then what about you? Can't you have the surgery?''

''I've decided against it.''

Rachel stepped back from him, looked at him as though he'd lost his mind. ''But why? If it means you could stay with the SEALs or…'' She frowned. ''Or is there some danger in the procedure?''

''There's some risk. There's about a 60 percent success ratio, but there's also a chance it won't work and my hearing could be worse.''

''Are we talking like total deafness in the ear if it fails?''

''No. Just slightly more diminished.''

''But I don't understand. If there's a good chance you could get your hearing back and remain with the SEALs, why wouldn't you have the surgery?''

Mac hesitated, searched for the right words to explain his decision. ''I told you, it doesn't fit in with my plans. Besides, why risk making the situation worse when there's no need to? The way I see it my hearing shouldn't be an obstacle in my getting a regular job. Thanks to my training, I should be able to find something in any number of fields.''

Rachel eyed him skeptically. ''I'm sure you'd have no problem finding a job. But why would you even want to when you already have the only job you've ever wanted?''

''Rachel, haven't you been listening? I want us to get married, be a family. But even without that, I've already explained that there's no place for me with the SEALs because I'm flawed. Flawed,'' he repeated, practically spitting the words out and wishing she would just drop it. ''I've accepted that fact, so why can't you? Or is it that you don't want someone who's flawed, either?''

Rachel whipped up her chin defiantly. She took a step toward him, poked her index finger in his chest. ''Don't try to lay that on me, Mac McKenna. I loved you two years ago. And though heaven only knows why, I still love you and probably always will.''

''Rachel…''

''Back off and let me finish,'' she commanded when he started to gather her close. ''I'm not buying it, Mac. Your reason for not having the surgery. You've never been afraid of taking risks. If anything, you thrive on it. So why the sudden act of cowardice on your part?''

''I told you, I just don't see the point in going through with the surgery. Anyway, it's not important. What is important is that there's nothing standing in the way of us getting married now.''

Rachel shook her head. ''I can't marry you, Mac.''

''But why?'' he asked, completely bewildered. ''You love me. You even admitted it a few minutes ago.''

''Yes, I do love you,'' she told him, and the look in her eyes was impossibly sad.

"And I love you. So what's the problem?"

"The problem is that you don't love me, Mac. Not really. Or at least not the way I want and deserve to be loved. If you did, you wouldn't be copping out the way you're doing. Because that's what you're doing by not having the surgery."

"My decision not to have the surgery has nothing to do with my feelings for you," he argued.

"You really don't see it, do you?"

"See what?" he asked, feeling as though he were swimming in quicksand.

"It's this crazy idea you've got about not being able to be a SEAL and having a family. You've convinced yourself that you can't have both, so by opting not to have the surgery, you don't really have to make a choice. The choice is made for you, and I win you by default."

"That's not true."

"Isn't it? Then why not have the surgery, Mac?"

"I've already explained."

Rachel shook her head. "You found an excuse. Because if you had the surgery and your hearing was restored, then there really wouldn't be any reason for you to resign from the SEALs. But do nothing and the decision is made for you. You can't remain with the SEALs, so it's okay to marry me. While I appreciate the offer, I'm not willing to settle for being your second choice."

"That's not true."

"Then prove it. Go through with the surgery, stay with the SEALs and marry me. Make a home with me and P.J."

"I can't do that, and it has nothing to do with you being my second choice. Even if I had the surgery and it was successful, I wouldn't stay with the SEALs—not and marry you. I told you, I won't put you through what my father put my mother and family through. You don't know what his death did to my mother. If he hadn't been selfish, if he had really loved her, he would have walked away the way I'm willing to do.''

''And maybe he didn't walk away because your mother loved him enough not to ask him to give up something that was so much a part of him. The way I never would have asked you to give up something that's so much a part of you.''

At a loss, Mac said, ''That's because you don't know the dangers, the risks involved. You don't know what it was like for my mother, always worrying, crying at night when she thought no one could hear her because she was so lonely for my father, so worried about him.''

''You're right. I don't know what it was like for your mother. But then, neither do you, Mac. Not really. You were just a child yourself.''

''I was old enough to see how unhappy he made her, how miserable she was when he died,'' Mac countered.

''But what about before he was killed? He must have also made your mother happy, too. Does she have all these regrets you seem to think she has?''

''I've never asked her,'' Mac replied. ''I didn't have to. I saw what she went through.''

''Maybe you didn't see things as clearly as you think you did because you were grieving yourself. Perhaps it's time you asked your mother, Mac. Ask her how she feels? Ask her whether or not, if she had it to do over, would she marry your father again. You might find yourself surprised by her answer.''

''Fine. If it makes you happy, I'll talk to my mother. But whatever she feels, it doesn't have anything to do with us. The point is I love you enough not to ask you to live with the kind of worry and loneliness she did.''

"You don't have to ask me—because you've made sure there is no choice to make."

"Rachel—"

"And what happens if you get hit by a car crossing the street? Or heaven forbid you're killed in a freak accident?"

"You're not making any sense. What does that have to do with my not having the surgery and resigning my commission?"

"Everything. And nothing," she said and sighed. "Loving someone is the real risk, Mac. Not whether or not you're a SEAL. Sure I would have worried about you whenever you left for a mission and I'd certainly have prayed you'd come back to me safely. But I'd have known you were doing what you wanted to do, what you loved to do. If you'd really loved me, you would have realized that I'd already taken the biggest risk of all by loving you."

"Then take another risk," Mac pleaded. "Marry me."

She shook her head. "I can't."

"Can't or won't?" he countered, feeling both hurt and angry at the rejection.

"Won't," she told him. "You were right two years ago. I deserve a man who truly loves me, a man who chooses a life with me instead of settling for one because he's afraid to go after what he wants. Most of all, I deserve a man who trusts that the love we share is strong enough to weather whatever comes our way. I wanted that man to be you, Mac. I'm truly sorry that it wasn't. Now you'll have to excuse me," she said with all the politeness he'd expect of a stranger and not a woman in whose bed he'd spent the night. "I have to go pick up P.J. from his sitter."

"Rachel, wait," he called out when she started to leave the room. " I love you. We can work this out."

She shook her head.

"What about P.J.?" he asked, panic settling in his gut.

"I won't try to keep you from P.J., Mac. You just let me know how much or how little you want to be involved in his life and we'll work it out."

"This discussion isn't over. I'm not going to let either one of you go," he called out to her retreating back. And somehow, he promised himself, he would make things right between them. He just had to figure out how.

"Daddy?" P.J. asked four days later at the sound of the front door opening. In his dark gray cords and bright blue sweater he made a clumsy attempt at racing across the kitchen toward the doorway.

"Sorry, slugger," Chloe said as she stepped into the room. "It's just Aunt Chloe."

She picked him up, gave him a snuggle and kiss.

"Daddy?" he asked again as he tried to look past her shoulder.

Rachel's throat tightened at her son's obvious longing for his father. She certainly understood. Even though she'd washed the sheets and any trace of Mac from her room, every time she closed her eyes she could see him there, remember what it was like to be with him.

"Daddy," P.J. demanded.

"Daddy's not here P.J. He…he had to go away for a little while. Here's your apple juice," she said, and Chloe put him down so that he could retrieve the sippy cup.

"Tookie?" he asked, looking up at her with those big blue eyes so like his father's.

"No cookies. It's almost time for dinner."

Chloe knelt down, whispered something in his ear that

made him giggle, then he went over to reclaim his stuffed
teddy that had been abandoned at the sound of the front
door opening.

"Any word from the commander?" Chloe asked.

Rachel shook her head. "After...after that last conversation we had, he spent some time with P.J. that morning and told me he'd be away for a few days."

"You know, honey, after that little scene you told me
about, he might have decided to have the surgery. Maybe
he's been in the hospital. I could call and—"

"I already did," Rachel admitted. "This morning. I...I
just had to know. I've never seen Mac so...so broken the
way he was when he left here."

"And?"

"And if he was there, he isn't there now."

"Well, did you ask if he'd been a patient recently?"
Chloe demanded.

"They wouldn't say. And who can blame them. I
mean, it's not like I'm his wife or even his girlfriend."

Chloe went to her, hugged her and stroked her hair as
if she was a child. "But you are the mother of his child,
and the woman who loves him. Oh, honey, that pride of
yours is going to choke you one day."

"You're one to talk," Rachel told her. Swiping at her
eyes, she made an effort to recover her composure. "Who
was in love with the boy next door her entire life, but
did everything she could to make the man think she dis-
liked him?"

Chloe sniffed at that. "I was hoping it was like the flu
and I'd get over him."

"And I suppose that's why you encouraged him to go
out with your best friend?"

"Hey, I didn't expect the stupid man to go through

some midlife crisis and decide it was time he find himself a wife,'' Chloe defended.

''Speaking of becoming a wife, how are the wedding plans coming?''

''Don't ask,'' Chloe replied. ''Between my mother and his, I'm about to go insane. In fact, I intend to spend this weekend trying to convince Alex to elope.''

Rachel gave her friend a hug, happy that at least one of them was looking at a bright future with the man she loved. ''I'm happy for you and Alex, Chlo. Truly.''

''I know. I wish things had worked out for you with the commander. I still can't believe he just gave up the way he did. I never would have pegged him as a quitter.''

''I don't think he is,'' Rachel said, quickly coming to Mac's defense. ''But to be fair, I didn't give him a lot of options. I don't want him by default. If he'd really loved me, he would have understood that.''

''Maybe you were too hard on him, honey. After all, he might have decided it was time for him to leave the Navy. The ear thing was just an excuse.''

''No,'' Rachel insisted. ''Mac loves being a SEAL. He once told me it wasn't just what he did, it was who he was. But he has that dumb hang-up about not being able to remain a SEAL and be married because of his father. If I had taken him up on his marriage proposal and let him resign, it would have killed a part of him. I couldn't do that. Besides, deep down I would always worry that the day might come when he'd regret his decision and hate me because of it.''

The doorbell sounded and P.J. began trying to push up to his feet from his position on the kitchen floor where he'd been playing with his teddy bear and a truck that Mac had given him. ''Daddy,'' he squealed, and started to scramble toward the door when the bell sounded again.

"I'm beginning to think the real mistake I made was letting him into P.J.'s life so easily. How am I ever going to explain to him if his daddy decides not to come back?" Scooping up her son, who had already tottered a few feet into the hall, she and Chloe headed toward the front door.

Chloe reached the door first, unlocked and opened it. "Well, well, well. Look who's back," Chloe said, and shot Rachel a knowing look.

"Daddy!"

When P.J. began squirming, Rachel put him down. He raced toward Mac, who she noted was wearing his dress uniform. The sight of him filled her with a mixture of relief and alarm.

"Hey, pardner," he said, his face lighting up when he spotted P.J. Stooping down, he held out his arms and swallowed P.J. up in them. "I missed you, pal," he told P.J. as he put him at arm's length.

"Miss you," her son echoed.

Mac plunked his hat down on P.J.'s head, then standing tall he saluted his son. When P.J. attempted to do the same, Rachel's throat grew thick with tears.

"Honestly, Petey. Am I going to have to wait all day to meet my grandson?"

Only then did Rachel look past Mac to see the slender, elegant woman standing at the door behind him. Mac's mother, Rachel realized, immediately noting the resemblance about the eyes.

"Sorry, Mom," Mac said, and stepped aside so that she could enter. "I'd like you to meet your grandson, Peter James. Commander P.J.," he continued. "This is your grandma Jane."

"Oh, he's beautiful, Petey. Just beautiful."

"Excuse me," Chloe said, coming forward. "I'm Chloe Chancellor."

The older woman stood, and, after wiping tears from her eyes, smiled and held out her hand to Chloe. "I'm pleased to meet you. I'm Jane McKenna, Petey's mother."

Ten

"**P**etey, huh?" Chloe said, and Rachel didn't have to see her friend's face to know that there was devilment dancing in her eyes. The look Mac shot Chloe promised retribution if she ever used the nickname. "What happened? Lose your key?"

Mac glared at Chloe. "Since I've been away for a few days, I thought it best to announce myself before just coming inside," he told her.

"And you, my dear, must be Rachel," Jane said, and made no attempt to hide her curiosity.

"Yes, ma'am, I am."

"I can't tell you how happy I am to finally meet you," she said, and when Rachel would have withdrawn from the handshake, the other woman leaned forward and gave her a hug. "Petey has told me so much about you. I feel as though I know you already."

Rachel shot her gaze to Mac who was watching her

intently. "I took your advice and went to see my mother, to get her perspective on a few things."

"I see," Rachel said cautiously, aware of their audience. And for the first time since Mac had walked out the door four days ago, Rachel began to think there was hope for them after all.

"Since it doesn't appear that Petey and my friend, here, are going to make it past the foyer anytime soon, Mrs. McKenna, would you like to come inside and sit down?" Chloe asked.

"Forgive me," Rachel said quickly, embarrassed to have been so caught up with Mac that she had momentarily forgotten his mother. "Please, come in. Can I offer you something to drink? Some tea perhaps. Or a soda or a cup of coffee?"

"Coffee would be lovely. Thank you."

"If you'll just follow me," Rachel began.

"Petey, could you get that present I brought for P.J. out of your truck?"

"Present?" P.J. repeated, his eyes lighting up.

"And Chloe, dear, I had Petey stop and pick up a poinsettia from the florist that I think would look lovely on your front porch. Perhaps you could show him where to put it?"

"Be happy to," her friend said.

Mac's gaze shot between his mother and her, Rachel noted, and when he failed to move despite P.J.'s tugging at him, Chloe hooked her arm in his. "Come on, Petey. Let's go get the plant."

"Witch," Mac muttered, and trotted outside with Chloe and P.J.

"Mac tells me that you're a nurse, my dear," Jane McKenna began.

"Yes, ma'am," Rachel replied, and led the older woman into the kitchen for the coffee she'd promised.

Ten minutes later Rachel tried to recall if she had ever been so expertly maneuvered and decided she had not. While she couldn't vouch for the type of woman Jane McKenna had been when Mac was growing up, the woman seated across from her at the kitchen table wasn't at all the fragile, helpless woman she had envisioned.

"Is something wrong, dear?" Jane asked her. "You look surprised."

"No. Not at all," Rachel told her, embarrassed to have been caught with her thoughts wandering. "I was just thinking you're not at all what I expected."

"I hope that's a good thing."

"Oh, it is," Rachel said, and quickly explained that she hadn't expected Mac's mother to be so strong.

Jane laughed at that. "I think my son was also surprised. He had a lot of skewed ideas about how his father's death affected me. He's so like his father—not just in his appearance and choice of profession, but in his thinking. My husband was a bullheaded man, and I'm afraid that Petey...Mac," she amended with a smile, "Mac's inherited his father's stubborn streak. Once he gets an idea in his mind, it's not easy getting him to change it."

"I know," Rachel admitted.

"Yes, I'm sure you do," she said, and retrieved one of the biscotti cookies from the dish Rachel had set on the table. "I just hope you love him enough not to give up on him."

Unsure what to say, Rachel remained silent.

"I'm sorry, Rachel," Mrs. McKenna said, and reached out to pat her hand. "I didn't mean to embarrass you. But it is fairly obvious that you're in love with him."

"Yes, I am. But sometimes love isn't enough."

"Take the word of someone who has known great love and had it snatched away quite suddenly. Love is the only thing that really matters. Don't waste a single minute of the time you can have with each other, dear, because neither of you has any way of knowing if that next day will be your last."

"You're talking about your husband. Mac told me how you lost him so quickly."

"Yes, I did," Mrs. McKenna told her, a sad look in her eyes. "I'm glad you suggested Mac talk to me about his father's death. As I said, he had some skewed ideas about how I felt, and thought I had regrets about marrying his father."

"Did you? Regret marrying him?" Rachel asked, unable to help herself.

"Never. Pete McKenna was one of the finest men I've ever known. Even though I only had him for a short time, I wouldn't trade one minute of the years that I did have with him for a lifetime with anyone else."

"You still love him," Rachel said, and tried to imagine what it was like to love someone that way even after he'd been dead twenty years. Surprisingly, she could, because she suspected she would love Mac the same way.

"Always. There's not a day that goes by that I don't think of him, that I don't miss him," she said, and toyed with the gold band on her left hand.

"How do you stand it?" Rachel asked.

"I lead a full life. I have my family and now, thanks to you, a lovely grandson." She flashed her that quick smile so like Mac's. "I also have a job I enjoy and good friends. And, of course, I have wonderful memories."

She had those same things—P.J., her family, good

friends and a job she loved. And she also had her memories of those magical times with Mac.

"You don't have to settle for memories yet," Mrs. McKenna said as though she could read her thoughts. "I hope for my son's sake and your own that you won't." She stood at the sound of voices and the front door slamming. Giving her another warm smile, she said, "Thank you for the coffee and the conversation."

"You're welcome," Rachel told her as she began clearing the table.

"Mom," Mac said as he came through the kitchen door, a warning note in his voice as he looked from his mother to Rachel and back again. "Don't you want to see P.J. playing with his truck?"

"Oh, I'd love to," Mrs. McKenna replied, and fled the room.

Alone with Mac for the first time since that scene several days ago, Rachel was at a loss as to what to say to him. Especially when she was feeling so emotional and conflicted after speaking to his mother.

"I hope she didn't grill you too badly," Mac finally said.

"She didn't. You're mother's a lovely woman. I like her."

"Thanks." And as though he too felt awkward, he jammed his hands into his pockets. "Listen, I'm sorry I just sprung her on you this way, but she insisted on coming. There was just no talking her out of it—even with the flights full because of the Thanksgiving holidays. If there hadn't been a cancellation at the last minute, I'd have been driving her here instead."

"I'd almost forgotten about tomorrow being Thanksgiving," Rachel said, more to herself than to Mac. She glanced at her watch, realized it was later than she'd thought. She was due at the hospital in less than thirty minutes. "Mac, I—"

"Rachel, I—"

They laughed. And Mac said, "You go first."

"I was just going to say that I…your ear," she said, only now noticing the wad of cotton when he turned his head slightly. "Is it giving you trouble?"

He reached up, touched his ear as though he hadn't realized the cotton was there. "Not for much longer, I hope. I had the surgery three days ago after talking to my CO."

"And your hearing? Is it okay?" she asked, afraid to even think what his going through the surgery meant about any future for them, given Mac's view of marriage and his career.

"I won't know for a while yet," he said with a smile that for the first time she thought was laced with nervousness. "But, hey, if it doesn't, I can always get fitted with a hearing aid. Right?"

"Right," she replied, and ached a little inside for him. But aware of the time clicking by, she said, "I'd like to hear about it…the surgery, that is. But I'm afraid I can't right now. I'm supposed to go on duty at the hospital in thirty minutes."

"Could you get someone to fill in for you? The surgery is only one of the things I wanted to tell you. I had a chance to do a lot of thinking these past few days while I was away. I came to a number of realizations about myself, some of them not very pleasant. I also made a number of decisions about my future, but I'd like to discuss them with you. So I was hoping that we could talk."

"I'd like that, Mac. I really would, and I feel especially bad because your mother's here, but I'm afraid the hospital's short-staffed because of the long holiday weekend.

I agreed to take an extra shift this evening so that I could have the long weekend to go to my parents'.''

"You mean you're going to be gone for the next four days?"

At the utter disappointment in his eyes, she relented. "That was my plan, but maybe I can make a few changes." She slanted a glance at her watch again and groaned. "But right now I really do have to get moving."

"How about me giving you a lift to work and picking you up at the end of your shift?"

"Sure," she told him. "As long as you don't mind having to wait until midnight to pick me up."

As a rule Mac didn't mind waiting. Patience was something he'd exercised often as a SEAL. Like the time he'd spent six hours in freezing water before executing a raid on gun smugglers. Or the time he'd remained crouched in a trench outside an enemy compound he'd been sent to bug from dawn until nightfall when the leader of the camp had returned unexpectedly. But the eight hours he'd had to wait for Rachel's shift to be over had surely been the most difficult of his life.

That's why he'd snatched up his keys and headed for the hospital a full forty-five minutes before he should have. Maybe he'd luck out and Rachel could sneak away a little early, he mused. There was so much he wanted to tell her, so much he wanted to explain. Above all, he wanted her to believe him when he said that he loved her, because he truly did. He also wanted to share his life with her and P.J. And if she was willing to take a chance on him, then so was he.

Lost in thought, he pulled into the visitor parking lot at the hospital. Exiting his truck, he started across the lot to the hospital before he sensed something was off. After a moment he realized that it was the quiet. It was too quiet, he decided. There were no employees hanging around outside the hospital taking a break or smoking a cigarette. No one was entering or leaving the hospital at all. While it was past visiting hours, there were always a few visitors who remained at the hospital longer, not to mention that the hospital staff was always coming and going as they changed shifts.

An uneasy feeling settled in his belly as he made his way across the street. Watching, assessing, he climbed the stairs at the front of the hospital to the entrance and frowned when he found the front door unlocked. He recalled Rachel telling him that as a security precaution, the doors were always locked after nine o'clock but that security guards patrolled the first floor corridors and could let someone in or out as needed.

Mac slipped inside. A quick look around the lobby entrance revealed no sign of a security guard. A scan of the elevator banks revealed all six cars to be stationary and empty. He checked the control panel, noted that all of the elevators had been programed to remain on the first floor, making them unavailable for use.

That uneasiness in his gut escalated to flat-out worry as Mac stepped back out into the cold night. Keeping to the shadows, he made his way around to the side of the building that housed the emergency room entrance, where Rachel had told him she'd be working tonight. A quick perusal of the entrance revealed lights blazing inside, phone lights blinking red at the admitting desk, but no sign of anyone.

With all of his senses on full alert, Mac checked the outside wall, noted the window positioned high up. Glad he'd opted for sneakers instead of his boots, he scaled the brick surface without making a sound. When he

reached the window that looked down into the large treat-
ment room that normally was partitioned off with privacy
screens for patients, he realized he'd been right to worry.

In a matter of seconds he assessed the situation, noting
that the screens had been either shoved into a corner or
knocked over onto the floor. Two men and a woman in
hospital gowns sat huddled in a corner with a nurse, an
orderly and what was apparently the admitting clerk. A
skinny, pock-faced punk in black jeans and jacket with
a gun in each hand kept pacing in front of them as he
kept watch over them. Two men in security guard uni-
forms lay slumped on the floor with their hands cuffed
behind their back and gags in their mouths. A clone of
the pock-faced punk, wearing the same black getup and
sporting an extra twenty pounds on his frame, stood
guard over the security team. The older of the two offi-
cers sported a nasty cut and bruising to his right temple
that Mac suspected was courtesy of a gun butt.

When he spotted Rachel, Mac's heart nearly stopped
in his chest. A wild-eyed, nervous kid who didn't look a
day over twenty had his arm locked around her throat in
a deadly grip and a 38 magnum pointed at her head. Rage
burned white hot in his veins and it took everything in
Mac not to break through the window and rip the kid into
pieces with his bare hands.

The punk shouted something, his face twisting in anger, and in his agitated state, he increased the pressure
on Rachel's throat. With the idiot in danger of crushing
her larynx, Mac decided he couldn't wait and was poised
to hurl himself through the glass window when Rachel
grabbed at the kid's arm with both hands and he finally
eased the pressure.

*Get a grip, McKenna. You need to save her not get
her killed.*

And for the first time in all his years as a SEAL, Mac found himself scared. At the flurry of movement, Mac sliced his gaze from Rachel to see what was causing the would-be Billy the Kid to put up such a fuss and spied the young doctor hovering over another man lying on the table. From the amount of blood staining the sheets and floor and the deep color, Mac suspected the hoodlum's pal was in a bad way. He'd had enough emergency first aid and seen enough wounds and blood out in the field to know when a hit was lethal. This one was, which meant the punk wasn't going to make it. He suspected the doc knew it, too. Probably the reason for the sweat across his brow and for the slight trembling of his fingers.

He had to get Rachel and the others out before trigger-happy Billy's buddy bought it. And whatever he did, he had to move fast. He jumped down from the wall, landing with a soft thud on the grassy surface and immediately set about checking the perimeter for another way in.

A check of the delivery entrance revealed he could gain entry in a matter of minutes—but not without some risk. Quickly he assessed the remaining points of entry and concluded that while he could probably get into the E.R. room, there was no way he could do so and overtake all three gunmen without putting Rachel or one of the other hostages at risk. Remembering the color and quantity of blood on the fellow on the table, he didn't have much time.

His best bet, Mac decided, was to forget trying for another means of access and walk right through the front door of the emergency room. If his luck held out and he did a decent job of faking an injury, he could take them by surprise. With that thought in mind, Mac sprinted around to the front, intent on putting his plan into action. But he'd no sooner turned the corner of the building than he spied the silent dark cars parked on the corner. Cops, he surmised, even though the cars weren't marked. Afraid that seeing him would set off some type of alarm and possibly a chase, Mac circled back around the building and came up behind one of the vehicles. He tapped on the darkened window and had to bite back a grin when the plainclothes detective jumped.

The window slid down revealing a none-too-happy guy. "Beat it, pal."

"You here because of the hostage situation in the hospital?"

The cop narrowed his dark eyes, causing silvering brows to squinch together. "What do you know about the hostage situation?"

"That my fiancée's inside and there's a trigger-happy punk holding a gun to her head. What can you tell me about the gunmen?"

"Listen, I'm sorry about your fiancée, son. But this is a police matter. We're working on getting her and the others out of there safely. The best thing you can do for her is to get out of here and let us do our job."

Losing patience, Mac said, "Okay, detective. Why don't we try this again. My name is Commander Pete McKenna, U.S. Navy SEALs, and the woman in there with a gun aimed at her head happens to be my future wife. I'm going in there to get her out. And if you know anything about the kid with the gun I'll be dealing with, it would help. But either way, I am going in there and getting my woman out."

"Hang on a second," the detective said. He exited the car. So did the younger detective. "Listen, Commander…"

"McKenna," Mac supplied the name.

"Hutchinson," the older man said. "That's Jones."

Mac nodded. ''We don't have much time. The guy on the table isn't going to make it. And when he buys it, things are going to get ugly. So what can you tell me about the gunmen?''

''We think it's the Boudreaux boys. Three brothers and a cousin. They're two-bit punks that run with a local gang called the Brotherhood. Until recently their MO has been petty larceny. A couple of weeks ago they started hitting a few convenience stores. They'd go in wielding guns, clean out the registers and take off. But about an hour ago we got a call saying someone matching their description had hit a mom and pop store. They pistol-whipped the owner's wife, cleaned out the register and were leaving when the woman's husband came out of the back of the store with a shotgun. Says he hit one of them before they got away.''

The kid on the table, Mac surmised. And a shotgun blast at that range explained the loss of blood and severity of the wound. ''Anything else?''

''Twenty minutes ago a call came in from the hospital. A nurse on one of the patient floors. She said a shooting victim had been brought in and had taken the E.R. staff hostages. They've shut down the elevators and sent word that if they so much as hear a police siren or see a cop, they'll begin shooting hostages—starting with the hospital employees and then the patients. A SWAT team is supposed to be on its way now. In fact, they should have been here by now.''

''We can't wait for them,'' Mac told him again. ''I've already checked for points of entry. The easiest access would probably be through the receiving area where they receive hospital supplies. But there's no way to get in without putting the hostages at risk. I'm going to go through the emergency entrance, pretend I'm sick, then try to take them by surprise and disarm them.''

''Are you out of your mind?'' Hutchinson asked. ''You'll be committing suicide. Not to mention what will happen to the others in there.''

''I know what I'm doing, Hutchinson.''

''Yeah? You said yourself there are three of them in there with guns and you're not even carrying a weapon. What are you going to do? Take them out with your bare hands?''

''And my feet,'' Mac told him, and couldn't help smiling when the other man's jaw literally dropped. He started down the street toward the parking lot to get his truck. The two detectives hurried behind him.

''McKenna, this is crazy. You'll never be able to pull it off,'' Hutchinson insisted.

Mac stopped, and the two guys nearly ran into him. ''Listen, I know what I'm doing, Hutchinson. I'm a U.S. Navy SEAL. I've been involved in countless rescue missions under circumstances a lot worse than these.'' But not one of those missions had ever meant as much to him personally.

''He's right, Hutch,'' Jones told his partner. ''I saw a special on these SEAL guys. They're supposed to be like super warriors.''

''This isn't a war,'' Hutchinson pointed out.

''No, it's not. But the woman I love is in there, and I intend to get her out. If you want to help, put one of your men on the east wall. There's a window there. Make sure he's quiet and isn't seen. He can monitor what goes down from there. Tell him when I give the signal to have the rest of your team move in.''

And before they could waylay him with more questions, Mac took off for his truck. It was ironic, he thought as he pulled the truck out of the lot and made a speeding entrance into the emergency-room lane. All the time he'd spent agonizing about possibly leaving his SEAL team, worrying that he couldn't commit to Rachel because he feared something would happen to him and he'd leave Rachel behind grieving. And now Rachel was the one in jeopardy and he was the one who might be left alone.

No way did he intend to let that happen, he promised himself as he mussed his hair, untucked his shirt. Shutting off the engine, he exited the truck, leaving the door open and faked a fall in the driveway. Only now when he was faced with losing her did he finally realize that he could live without being a SEAL. He could live without being able to hear. What he couldn't...wouldn't live without was Rachel.

And with that thought in mind, he hugged his gut, hunched over and stumbled into the emergency shouting, "Help! Someone help me!"

Rachel sucked in a breath at the sound of his voice. And she knew even before the man came stumbling into the room where she and the others were being held hostage that it was Mac.

"What the—Get the hell out of here," the guy holding her, called Mick, yelled.

"Help me. You've got to help me," Mac cried out and gave all the signs of a man in severe pain. "It's my stomach. I think...I think I've got food poisoning."

"Buddy, you're going to have a belly full of lead if you don't turn around and get out of here. Now!"

"Then go ahead and shoot me," Mac told him, and winced as though he were in severe pain. "Anything's got to be better than this." And in a move that would have done the most ardent acting coach proud, he stumbled over and fell at Mick's feet.

Rachel could feel the shock go through Mick. He jerked the gun barrel away from her temple and aimed it at Mac, which had her heart all but jump in her throat. She was barely conscious that the arm he'd kept anchored around her throat had loosened.

Mick nudged Mac with his foot, and Rachel had to bite back a wince at the sound of his shoe connecting with Mac's rib. Not that it seemed to bother Mac, who lay on the floor, his arms wrapped around his middle, and gave every impression that he was out cold.

"Sammy, get over here and get rid of this guy," Mick yelled.

"Maybe…maybe I should see if I can help him," Rachel offered.

Mick tightened his arm around her throat again. "He's not your concern," he told her.

"Come on, Sammy. Get over here."

"What about the guards?" Sammy asked, his gaze shifting from Mick back to the two trussed guards he held at gunpoint.

"They'll be all right," Mick assured his partner. "Jimbo," Mick called to the other gunman. "If either of those guys move, shoot them."

Under other circumstances she would have found the scenario funny, Rachel thought as she watched Sammy try to lift a supposedly unconscious Mac off the floor to throw him out.

"Come on, Sammy. What's the problem? Get the guy out of here before he wakes up," Mick ordered.

Sammy wiped sweat from his brow. "I can't do it by myself. Either you or Jimbo need to help me. The dude's bigger than he looks, and he weighs a ton."

Actually Mac was at least four inches taller than the three desperadoes, as she thought of them. He also had a good forty pounds on the thinner Sammy.

"Jimbo, come give Sammy a hand."

"What about them?" he asked, waving his gun toward the patients and three hospital employees.

"They'll be all right. Hurry up, come help Sammy."

Jimbo joined Sammy, and while one of them started to lift Mac's shoulders and the other his feet, everything seemed to happen at once. Lightning quick, Mac's feet and hands were flying. His foot connected with Sammy's head, sending him flying into a wall and slumping to the floor while he karate-chopped Jimbo at the neck and sent the bigger man sliding down in a puddle of humanity. Mac spun his body, and Rachel heard bone snap when Mac's foot kicked Mick's hand and sent the gun flying across the floor.

"Get back or I'll snap her neck," Mick yelled and tightened his good arm around her throat.

Mac froze. "Let her go. You want a hostage? Take me."

Mick laughed, but she could smell the fear on him. "I like the hostage I've got. Now back off and or I'll kill her. I swear it," he said, and to prove his point he increased the pressure on her neck.

Rachel choked. She clutched at the powerful arm threatening to cut off her breathing.

"All right," Mac said, and took a step back. He held up his hands. "I'm backing off. Just don't hurt her."

"So, she's your woman, huh?" Mick countered, a cockiness in his voice.

"She's my life," Mac told him.

There was something in the way he said it, in the way

he looked at her, and Rachel knew he meant it. He really did love her.

"Your life, huh? Then I guess if I was to squeeze a little tighter and cause her to stop breathing, you'd die right along with her, wouldn't you?"

"You do anything to hurt her, you so much as cause her to chip a fingernail," Mac said, his voice deadly calm, his eyes ice cold. "And I swear, I'll make you wish you'd never been born."

Rachel felt the shudder of fear race through Mick's body, which made his grip around her neck tighten again. She pried at the arm, afraid if she didn't hold him back, he'd kill her without even trying.

"Hey, wh-who do you think you are, threatening me? I-I'm the one holding the hostage here, pal. I'm the one who gives the orders."

"It wasn't a threat, pal," Mac said, and even though she hadn't thought it possible, his voice sounded even calmer, colder. "It was a promise."

Another ripple of fear went through Mick, and the arm around her throat increased its pressure. She had to do something, Rachel decided. She thought of Mac, of P.J., of the life that they could have together. She had to take a chance. She had to let go of the arm crushing her neck and try to get free before he cut off her breath. Saying a silent prayer, she dropped her hands from the arm around her throat and immediately felt the pressure block off the air to her windpipe. Even as she gasped for breath, she drove her elbows into his gut.

It was all the opening Mac needed. He sent a fist flying at Mick's face. Mick released her as he cried out in pain and went stumbling back against the wall. Then there were policemen everywhere, cuffing a sobbing Mick, rounding up his partners.

"Rachel, are you all right?" Mac asked, gathering her into his arms.

She nodded and gulped in air.

"That was a brave thing you did, love, but very stupid," he chided. "What would I have done if he'd killed you?"

"He didn't," Rachel assured him. She put her fingers to his cheek, touched by the concern in his voice, his eyes.

"But he might have," he told her and kissed the hand that rested on his cheek. "You're my life, Rachel. You and P.J. Without you, nothing else matters." He hugged her close, crushing her to his chest.

"Mac, I'm all right," she tried to assure him.

"I know. But for a minute there..."

"I'm fine," she told him again. "But I would like to go home."

"That I can arrange," he said, and after speaking a few minutes with a silver-haired man she heard someone call Hutch, Mac led her outside.

She breathed in deeply, drinking in the cool, crisp night air. Looking up at the sky, she spied a shooting star, closed her eyes and made a wish. "I just realized something," she said. "It's Thanksgiving Day."

"You're right," he told her. "And I for one am feeling very thankful. You ready to go home?"

"Yes."

After opening the door of his truck for her, he climbed in the other side behind the steering wheel and started the engine. Turning to her, he asked, "You sure you're all right? That you don't want to see a doctor or something?"

His nerves warmed her heart. "I'm fine—except for one problem."

"What?"

"You saved my life tonight. And as I understand it when someone saves your life, you owe it to them. So now that my life belongs to you Commander, what do you plan to do with it?"

Mac grinned at her. "Well, P.J. was complaining to me about not having any little brothers or sisters to play with. So I sort of promised him that we'd get married and work on the baby part. I figure if I keep you naked and make love to you every chance I get, it might work."

"And this is all P.J.'s idea, huh?"

"Actually, he and I discussed the brothers and sisters part. The keeping you naked and making love to you part was all my idea."

"Why am I not surprised?" she asked.

He drove the car out toward the exit. When he reached the corner, he put it in Park and turned to her. "So what do you say, Rach? Will you marry me and let me spend the next fifty or so years of my life showing you how much I love you?"

"What about the SEALs, Mac?

"If the surgery is successful, I'd like to stay on. If the hearing loss is permanent, then I've already talked to my CO. There are other jobs I can do—not the same and not with my team—but I don't have to resign. But what I do depends on you."

"You mean if I agree to marry you, you'll resign regardless of what happens with the surgery," Rachel replied, disappointed that Mac still felt the need to choose. She couldn't help fearing that someday he would regret the decision and his choosing her.

He tipped up her chin. "No, that's not what I mean. I want both. But whether I stay in the Navy depends on how you feel about being married to a SEAL."

Her heart swelled in her chest. "I love you, Mac. And I'd be lying if I said I wouldn't worry about you and I'd miss you like crazy when you're away. But I would be all right about it because it's who you are, what you want to do."

"What I am is desperately in love with you. And what I want and need most in the world is you," he told her.

"You have me, Mac. You always have."

"And as long as I do, as long as I know that you love me, that I have you and P.J. waiting for me when the mission is over, that's all the reason I need to make sure I make it home safely." He kissed her gently on the lips. "So what do you say, Ms. Grant? Do we have a deal? Will you marry me?"

"We've got a deal, Commander."

* * * * *

Turn the page for a sneak preview of

BEHIND THE MASK

*the riveting new novel by Metsy Hingle
on sale in August 2002 from
MIRA Books.*

One

"I'll pay you one million dollars to find my wife."

"All right," Michael Sullivan replied from the other end of the phone line. "You've got my attention."

Adam Webster smiled in satisfaction at the ex-cop's change in attitude. "I'm glad to hear that," he said as he gazed at the view of the Miami skyline afforded him from his penthouse suite of offices. He was glad, but he wasn't at all surprised. He'd learned a long time ago that money talked—even to a man like Sullivan. A man who, according to his source, had been among Houston's best and brightest police detectives five years ago when he'd resigned abruptly following his partner's death in a drug bust that had gone wrong. Now he hired himself out as a detective, bodyguard or bounty hunter—whatever the situation called for. The man was said to be as mean as a rattlesnake and twice as dangerous. He also reportedly had the instincts of a bloodhound when it came to tracking down someone who didn't want to be found. It was Sullivan's latter skill that he needed now to find Lily. "You've been a difficult man to get in touch with, Sullivan," Adam said, making no attempt to hide his displeasure. "My assistant tells me she's left you several messages."

"I've been out of town finishing up a case. The only reason you caught me now is because I had to swing by to pick up some reports I needed for the case I'm working on."

"I see," Adam said tightly. "I'm not accustomed to being ignored, Mr. Sullivan."

"No one's ignoring you, Webster. But since I'm pressed for time, why don't we dispense with my lack of manners, and you tell me why you're willing to pay me a million dollars to find your wife."

"Because she's missing," Adam said sharply, angered by the man's insolence. Biting back his temper, he reminded himself that he needed Sullivan to find Lily. With temper making him edgy, he turned away from the sweep of windows and stalked over to his desk. Sitting down, he picked up the framed photo of Lily. "I understand your expertise is finding people. I'd like to hire you to find my wife."

"How long has she been missing?" Sullivan asked.

"Six months." And after six months it still gnawed at him like a festering sore that he had underestimated Lily as he had. He detested mistakes, refused to tolerate them. Yet he had made a mistake in not anticipating Lily's reaction.

Never in a million years would he have believed that sweet, docile Lily—the girl he'd fed, clothed and molded into a woman worthy to be his wife—would have the guts to defy him. To steal his gun. To shoot him. Even more infuriating was the fact that she'd not only gotten away from the idiots he'd hired to guard her, but that he'd doled out a considerable sum of money to private detectives and some not-so-reputable business associates to find her. And though they'd come close to grabbing her twice, she had still managed to get away. But not for much longer, Adam promised himself. If Sullivan was half as good as the reports indicated, Lily's rebellion was about to come to an end.

"Webster? You still there?"

"Yes. Yes," Adam repeated, dragging his thoughts back to the present. "What did you say?"

"I asked if you've filed a missing persons report?"

"No," Adam advised him. "I don't want the police involved."

"Why not?"

"Aside from the fact that I can do without the publicity, I don't want any charges filed against my wife."

"Last I heard, it wasn't a crime for a woman to leave her husband," Sullivan informed him.

"No. But shooting me, kidnaping my son and stealing cash and jewelry from my safe *are* crimes. If I had brought the police into it, they would have issued an arrest warrant for Lily. I'd prefer to handle things myself."

Sullivan swore.

"My sentiments exactly," Adam told him.

"How old's your boy?"

Adam frowned a moment while he calculated how old the kid would be now. "Two."

"Damn! That's got to be rough, him being so little and you missing all that time with him."

"It is," Adam said, because it was obvious that Sullivan expected it. But in truth, he didn't give a damn about the brat. He never had. As far as he was concerned his problems with Lily began with the kid. Not insisting that she terminate the pregnancy had been a major screwup on his part—one he would make sure didn't happen again. But first...first he had to get Lily back. "I'd like you to start looking for them right away, Mr. Sullivan. If you'll come by my office, say, within the hour, I'll provide you with any other information you'll need and give you a retainer for your services."

"I'm afraid I can't make it today."

Adam scowled. "Why not?" he demanded, unaccustomed to having his requests denied.

"Because at the moment I'm handling a matter for another client."

"And is this other client offering to pay you a million dollars for your services?" he demanded.

"No."

"Then I suggest you tell him or her to find someone else."

"That's not the way I work," Sullivan said, his voice dropping to a chilling growl. "When I commit to do a job, I do it. I've got to go. I'll give you a call when I get back, and if you're still interested in hiring me, we'll talk."

When the dial tone buzzed in his ear, Adam slammed down the telephone receiver. "Arrogant bastard," he muttered, clenching his hands into fists. Sullivan would pay for that, he promised. As soon as the man found Lily for him, he would make him regret his insolence. Shoving away from the desk, he headed to the bar and poured himself a shot of bourbon. He tossed it back, felt its sting as it slid down his throat to his gut like liquid fire. After pouring himself another one, he grabbed the crystal tumbler and stalked across the ultramodern office that he'd spent a small fortune decorating. Ignoring the polished finish on the black marble desktop, he set down his glass and picked up the silver-framed picture of Lily again. He stared at her—the pale, delicate skin, the silky blond hair—and felt the violent punch of lust. Reaching for the bourbon, he tossed back another swallow and all the while continued to stare at Lily's face.

Lily belonged to him. She had from the moment he'd first set eyes on her. Even at fifteen and still an innocent she'd left him breathless and aching. She'd been worth ten of her mother. It was the reason he'd saved her. Were it not for him, she'd have probably hooked up with some two-bit punk and been selling herself on the streets of Miami before she'd turned sixteen.

Instead, he'd rescued her from her wretched life. He'd provided for her education, showered her with gifts and when she'd been legally an adult he had married her. He hadn't had to make Lily his wife to bed her, Adam reasoned. Any number of women would have killed to be in her position, just for the chance to be in his bed. He knew he looked good, Adam admitted. He took care of himself, kept his body in shape and could easily pass for twenty years younger. Hadn't he heard a woman in one of his clubs call him a stud just last week? He could have had his pick of women to marry, but he'd chosen Lily. Lily. His breath turned to a pant as he thought of taking Lily that first time, of thrusting himself into her warm, tender flesh. And the memory made the throbbing in his groin even more painful.

He slapped down the glass and reached for the phone. "Kit, it's Adam," he said when the line was answered at the Miami nightclub. "How's that new girl working out, the young blonde with the southern drawl you introduced me to last week?"

"You must mean Annabelle," Kit said, her voice cool and sultry. "She's working out fine. A little shy, but the customers seem to like her. She's a fast learner and very eager to please. She should be here in a few minutes."

"Send her up to the penthouse when she gets there," he said, already anticipating the feel of the pretty, young girl beneath him. "And, Kit, get someone else to take her shift tonight. She's going to be busy."

After hanging up the phone, he reached for his glass and started to go to the bedroom adjoining his office to wait for Annabelle. But his gaze fell on Lily's photo again. He lifted his glass in a mock salute. "It won't be long now, Lily," he whispered before downing the remainder of the whisky. He would use Sullivan to find her, and once he had her back, he'd see to it that Lily never dared to defy him again.

As for Sullivan, the man was in need of a lesson in respect—which he personally intended to see that he got.

January 2002
THE REDEMPTION
OF JEFFERSON CADE
#1411 by BJ James

Don't miss the fifth
book in BJ James'
exciting miniseries
featuring irresistible
heroes from Belle Terre,
South Carolina.

February 2002
THE PLAYBOY SHEIKH
#1417 by Alexandra Sellers

Alexandra Sellers
continues her sensual
miniseries about
powerful sheikhs
and the women
they're destined
to love.

March 2002
BILLIONAIRE
BACHELORS: STONE
#1423 by Anne Marie Winston

Bestselling author
Anne Marie Winston's
Billionaire Bachelors prove they're
not immune to the power of love.

MAN OF THE MONTH

Some men are made for lovin'—and you're sure to love
these three upcoming men of the month!

Available at your favorite retail outlet.

Visit Silhouette at www.eHarlequin.com   SDMOM02Q1

Bestselling author
CAIT LONDON
**brings you another captivating book
in her unforgettable miniseries**

*One Western family finds the love that
legends—and little ones—are made of.*

Available in February 2002:
TALLCHIEF: THE HUNTER
Silhouette Desire #1419

Return to Tallchief Mountain as Adam Tallchief claims his
heritage and the woman he is destined to love. After twenty-
two years, Adam has come home to the family he didn't
know he has. But his old love and enemy, Jillian Green O'Malley,
is back, as well, and the passion that has always blazed
between them threatens to consume them both....

"Cait London is an irresistible storyteller."
—Romantic Times Magazine

Available at your favorite retail outlet.

Where love comes alive™

Visit Silhouette at www.eHarlequin.com   SDTALL